WROTTEN
ENGLISH

If you find any more examples of *Wrotten English*
let us know at the address below.

This edition published in 2011 in the United Kingdom by
Portico Books
10 Southcombe Street
London
W14 0RA

An imprint of Anova Books Company Ltd

The author has made every reasonable effort to contact all copyright holders. Any errors that may have occurred are inadvertent and anyone who for any reason has not been contacted is invited to write to the publishers so that a full acknowledgement may be made in subsequent editions of this work.

First published in Great Britain as *A Slip of the Pen* in 2004.

A CIP catalogue record for this title is available from the British Library.

ISBN 9781907554100

Typeset by SX Composing DTP, Rayleigh, Essex.

Printed and bound by Everbest Printing Co Ltd, China

This book can be ordered direct from the publisher at www.anovabooks.com

WROTTEN ENGLISH

A CELEBRATION OF LITERARY
MISPRINTS, MISTAKES AND MISHAPS

PETER HAINING

PORTICO

When once the itch of literature comes over a man,
nothing can cure it but the scratching of a pen.
Samuel Lover (1797–1868)

From this it is clear how much the pen is worse than the sword.
Robert Burton (1577–1640)

CONTENTS

INTRODUCTION

Recently I came across a quote by the sixteenth-century French essayist Michel Montaigne in his article 'Of Experience', which said, 'There are more books upon books than upon any other subject.' That is a pretty daunting thought when you are about to add another to the list almost five hundred years later. The truth is, of course, that every generation has loved its books, from the classics to contemporary fact and fiction, and when we are not reading them, what is more interesting than discussing them and their authors? Certainly the act of literary creation demands talent, energy and dedication – Douglas Adams, the late and much-lamented author of *The Hitchhiker's Guide to the Galaxy*, once referred to the process as 'staring at a blank piece of paper until your forehead bleeds'. Louis de Bernières, whose bestseller *Captain Corelli's Mandolin* made him wealthy and famous, offered an even stranger piece of verbal imagery. 'Writing today,' he said, 'is like being stood naked in Trafalgar Square and being told to get an erection.'

Behind the humour of both remarks there is a very real acknowledgement that authorship is bloody difficult, demands a big effort and is full of pitfalls and pratfalls – not the least of them the errors that can occur between the author's manuscript and the published work. That is what *Wrotten English* is all about.

During my writing career, spanning almost half a century as a newspaper reporter, journalist, publisher and author, I have had a passion for collecting the misdemeanours, unintentional or otherwise, of my chosen profession. And as a result of those years scouring the printed page I have been able to assemble a collection of authors' errors, publishers' boobs, printers' devils, double entendres, comic first lines, weird titles, literary graffiti and howlers, mistranslations, critics' gaffes and all manner of slip-ups committed to paper since the days of Montaigne and even earlier. Indeed, even in this modern age of e-book readers, iBooks and digital printing presses mistakes are still being made. Just ask US author Jonathan Franzen whose most recent novel *Freedom* was published – over 80,000 copies in the UK alone – with many 'typos and punctuation errors', leaving publishers HarperCollins blushing for simply not printing the final edited manuscript.

Bestselling contemporary author Terry Pratchett, whose *Discworld* novels made him a household name, has been asked countless times where he gets the ideas for his books. Terry typically replies, 'There's this warehouse called Ideas Are Us . . .' My answer would be in this instance less tongue-in-cheek and more straightforward. *Wrotten English* has come from many of those books Montaigne mentioned – as well as a lifetime devoted to reading about books and their authors. I am very grateful to them all.

I hope you enjoy this book as much as I enjoyed putting it together.

Peter Haining

ONE

STRANGE WHISKERS IN THE EAR

Typos and Other Tragedies

If I tell you that when my very first story was published some fifty years ago, it was full of literals, the title was changed and – to make things worse – even my name was spelt wrongly, you will no doubt understand why I have had a life-long interest in printers' errors, publishers' mistakes and slips of the writer's pen. Of course, when I became a young newspaper reporter in the 1950s, I soon learned just how easy it was for such errors to occur.

You have only to glance at the keyboard of a typewriter or computer to see how, for example, one wrong touch on the top line, QWERTYUIOP, and you can be in a whole world of trouble, especially with certain words, as the pages of this book will reveal time and again. The mistake can be compounded if it slips by an editor and then past the typesetter. In days of yore, typesetting machines produced lines of text from hot metal and if the compositor made an error there was no going back – no rubber, no Tipp-Ex, no computer spell-check to rite the rong. The whole line had to be reset and the old 'slug' (as they were appropriately named) consigned to the melting pot. On a great many occasions, though, they slithered into print...and then the fun began.

Collecting newspaper misprints is certainly not a new pursuit. As long ago as 1884, Frederic Williams, a London journalist with a wicked sense of humour, produced a little book, *Journalistic Jumbles: or, Trippings in Type*, which he subtitled, 'Being Notes on some Newspaper Blunders, their Origin and Nature' and included numerous examples, with a typical Victorian's eye for decency. Another newspaperman, W W Scott, had no such inhibitions when in 1931 he produced *Breaks*, 'A Collection of Mistakes and Misprints by those associated with the

Newspaper, Magazine and Book Racket'. A copy of this volume with its comical illustrations by Nate Collier was given to me on the day I became a journalist by an uncle who was a second-hand book dealer. It was probably intended as a salutary warning, but it certainly provided hours of amusing reading. Later still, in the 1950s, another whimsical fellow, Denys Parsons, followed in the footsteps of Williams and Scott and continued to scour the pages of national and local newspapers to compile a number of collections during the next thirty years.

Although I worked on a newspaper and then a London trade journal during the early years of my career, my particular interest was always in the spelling mistakes and typos in short stories and books – the area of publishing in which I hoped eventually to work.

Consequently, it was the faux pas of authors, the literals that somehow escaped the blue pencils of sub-editors, and the gibberish perpetrated by printers that caught my eye, and it is the best of these amusing and often risqué misprints that form this opening chapter...

After having given vent to this beautiful reflection, Mr Pickwick proceeded to put himself into his clothes; and his clothes into his portmanteau.

Charles Dickens, *Pickwick Papers*

Time had rolled back a hundred years.
People hurrying office-wards in the Strand
waved their hats and raised a cheer to the
immoral memory of Mr Pickwick.

Arthur Ramsey, *London Tapestry*

The Nolotic race is remarkable for the disproportionately long legs of their women. They extend on the eastern side of the Nile right down into the Uganda Protectorate.

Max Pemberton, *Strange Travels in Strange Places*

I was terrified. There was the tiger crouching, ready to bounce.

Fred M White, 'An Object Lesson'

His disappointment was keen, yet in after days he looked upon the evening as that date on which he burst from the chrysalis and became a caterpillar.

E Lynn Linton, *The World Well Lost*

'I didn't know that you cared for me that way,' she said. 'I've always thought of you as just a great big bother.'

Jean Ingelow, *Lost and Won*

She picked up a snapshot of a dear friend who had recently died on her bedroom mantelpiece.

Kate Field, 'A Woman's World'

For the chief the word compromise had no meaning. He answered his men in violet language.

Frederick Boyle, *A Story of the Transvaal*

Mrs Gale patted his arm affectionately. 'Don't forget,' she said, 'Come and hook me up next Thursday.'

Thomas Arthur, 'The Wayward Wife'

With an effort, Jean pulled herself together. She stopped crying and dried her ears.

Helen Mathers, 'A Summer Girl'

'Mr Perkins might be able to help you,'
she said, as she took down a dusty lodger
from the shelf.

James Payn, *Winifred's Lovers*

—•—

'Why are you here today, Mr Lomax?' Alice
stumbled over the familiar name. Mark reached
out his hand to help her to her feet.

Marjorie Bowen, 'My Lady Played'

—•—

I must say that when at last the house was
completed, it was an awful shack to us.

Marian Carter, *The Retreat*

—•—

There were two sharp reports and Radley lunched
and staggered.

Wilson McCoy, *The G-Man*

—•—

When he refused to give any evidence
to the police he was charged with assault and
carrying a gnu.

Frank Holderness, *The Silent Stranger*

The skipper spat disconsolately down
the engine-room ventilator and stopped the engines.

W W Jacobs, *Dangerous Waters*

They had hardly got into the skipper's cabin
when a tremendous pitch on the steamer sent Leila
rolling on the floor. Before she could be got under
control again she had shipped hundreds of tons
of water. Then her nose went down and her tail
went up and for a moment it was a question if
she would right herself.
A wiggle and a roll and she saved herself.

Albert Wetjen, *Afloat*

'If you ask me,' said Doris, 'it's more
like twelve years they have been married.
I don't think they will ever have a
chill now.'

Eleanor Stuart, 'The Right Man'

My father was born in poor circumstances, but he
did a rich man.

Katherine Tynan, *A Bit of a Scandal*

From his left ear to the corner of his mouth ran a
long scar, the result of a duet many years before.

William le Queux, *Flight from Germany*

For a moment he stood there looking into her eyes.
Between them was a bowl of hyacinths.

Elizabeth Robins, *Under the Southern Cross*

'The Duchess still looks quite a girl,' she said, 'and so does the Duke, particularly now that he has shaven off his tiny moustache!'

Louis Cohen, 'The Mayfair Set'

He leaned his head against her hair.
A wasp strayed across his face. He kissed it.

Alison Bold, *Moments to Cherish*

Pierre fingered one of his ears caressingly and looked thoughtfully at the other.

Paul Renin, *One Night in Paris*

Then it spread to Liz, who clapped a hand over her mouth above blue eyes that watered with silent laughter.

Henry Green, *Nothing*

She covered her face with her hands and cried brokenly. But, coming closer, he put both hands on her shoulders and lifted her tea-stained face to his.

Marilyn Foster, 'A Heart on Fire'

John Godfrey gathered the pale and wistful face into one hand, crumpling it up ridiculously, then he kissed it all over, released it and put her head back on his waistcoat, smoothing her rumpled hair.

Raymond Ellis, *The Girl from the Country*

Their house was full of little birds and I can see them to this day sitting on the sofa, holding hands and beaming.

Beth Cheney, *A Rural Idyll*

The eminent statistician rubbed his ear thoughtfully and produced a cigarette.

W Clark Russell, 'In Troubled Times'

She stood at the foot of the stairs, narrowing her eyes and breathing deeply through her hips.

Jennifer Mason, *The Moment is Past*

Deeply troubled, he wrote a poem about the war and the fighting hen.

William J Ford, *One Brave Soldier*

It wasn't the proper doctor – just a young locust taking his place while he was away.

Felix Barker, 'Heartbreak Hospital'

'You look a bit washed out, Bill,' said Doreen. She walked across the room and put her arm through him.

John Oxenham, *The Black Opal*

She sat huddled in a chair, covering her
ears with crossed legs.

Edgar Jepson, 'The Moment of Truth'

As he uttered the important word he dropped his
voice, but she just managed
to catch it.

Amy Ferguson, *The Unexpected Witness*

Raymond was perfectly happy.
He loved this woman with a great
and growling love.

Ian Maclaren, 'A Glasgow Drama'

The faces of the two men were livid with rage as she
quietly crumpled them up and threw them on the
fire.

Ella Fuller Maitland, *Christmas Expectations*

It was one of those perfect June nights that so seldom occur except in August.

Frankfort Moore, 'Reggie's Rival'

Miss Sutton struck out in all directions and the nurses called for help. However, when Dr Jackling arrived she had been overpowered.

Winifred Holtby, *Nothing to Fear*

The half-starved man sat down at the rough deal table and began to eat it ravenously.

Anthony Hope, *Bad Matches*

Anne crept cautiously up the stairs and knocked timidly at the door with the jelly.

Violet Hunt, *Window on the World*

He put the melting honey-coloured fruit on her plate and got out a silk handkerchief. She began to eat it thoughtfully.

F C Phillips, 'Romance for the Chambermaid'

Later that same evening after a vain search all around the village, Mary found the dog dead in the garden. She curried the body indoors.

Patricia Cox, *Life in Barnsthorpe*

She was sorry she had agreed to sleep in the haunted house, because all night long she was troubled by strange whiskers in her ear.

Edith A Barnett, 'The Haunted House'

Ted could not raise the cash necessary to purchase a house, and eventually in desperation he had to burrow.

Rosemary Jeans, *The Price of Love*

They looked out of the window as the train drew into Crewe station. 'Hull!' they cried, 'we're there.'

David Partridge, 'The Thompsons' Holiday'

The *Phyllida* throbbed with whispering engines to the shining, wet landing stage. Thorne caught her lightly and half lifted her ashore. 'By Jove, you're wet!' he said.

Stanley Weyman, *Phyllida*

'I am certain of one thing. Whatever may come between us – and wherever he may be on earth – Arthur will always remember that I love ham.

Millicent Hemming, *The Parting*

She had a pleasant voice, more like her smile than her sneer, but the man was frightened by an English voice and he submerged himself in his soup.

Warwick Deeping, *Restitution*

I never went through that ghastly
adolescent phase most girls experience.
I went from child to woman in one go.
One day I was a child. The next a man.

Patricia Gowling, 'A Hard Woman'

Sir Harry had his top lip caught under
his lower teeth.

W L Alden, *The Precedent*

My teeth were chattering as with a fever chill, when
they all tumbled out.

Roy Trevor, *The Deserted Wood*

Marjorie would often take her eyes from the deck
and cast them far out to sea.

Ursula Bloom, *A Voyage of Discovery*

He bent swiftly and found her lips and, without removing them from her mouth, lifted her to her feet and drew her into his arms.

Sonia Deane, *There Is a Destiny*

———

The door opened and a girl came in – a slip of a girl with a firm little chin and a pair of lively grey ewes which gave Bernard a searching glance.

Thomas Prescott, *The Guardian*

———

Alice paused and, to hide her confusion, busied herself adjusting ornaments on the mantelpiece which needed no adjustment. Then she turned her sweet, flour-like face towards him.

Marjorie Golden, 'Uncertainty'

———

He had been aware from the first that she was unusually attractive. Now, in her dark green dress with the low-cut, rounded neckline, he saw that she had lovely legs.

G H Coxe, *The Jade Venus*

Once again for an instant she raised those wonderful eyes to his. He studied the thickness of the lashes as they fell once more to her lap.

Barbara Cartland, *Love Will Triumph*

The doctor looked closely at the woman's face. 'It's a most peculiar thing,' he murmured.

Winifred Tanner, 'Reflections'

Elizabeth found herself on a stool by the nursery fire. Securely pierced by a long brass toasting fork she held a square of bread to the glowing flameless fire.

Jane MacDonald, *The Tides of Love*

He said he had a full and exciting wife.

James Edmunds, *The Story of Tom*

The lady in the thin black dress and a widow's veil, turned away and with a curling lip began to turn over a book lying on a table near her.

Roland James, 'The Mystery at Fetters'

Involuntarily, Max's eyes followed the length of the prostrate form, then uttered a piercing scream.

Peter Preston, *The Girl in the Club*

What was the meaning of all that apparatus? Racks of test tubes, most of them half-full; the microscopes on stands; the Bunsen burners; the white-painted box, on which was the word Incubator – what were these things? In a flash of intuition, Creighton realised the truth.
He was in a laboratory.

James Corbett, *The Somerville Case*

'The cause of death is a mystery,' the detective said,
'no doctor was attending him at the time.'

Frank McShane, 'With Murder in Mind'

In one corner of the room, square tins of
every shape were piled.

Edgar Wallace, *The Talkative Burglar*

'Today,' she said, and he held up a thumb and
grinned at her. If only this could be for ever, the two
of them alone. But the sea lifted the boat like a sullen
cork and he stopped thinking about anything but
handling her.

Richard Miles, *Exiled to the Pacific*

He glanced at May. She wasn't knitting, but sat
there, looking down at the floor, with knitted brows.

W Somerset Maugham, 'The Hour Before the Dawn'

The three girls spent several days at home with their mother. It was the first time the neighbours had the pleasure of seeing them in the altogether at one time.

Flora A Steel, *Long Island Days*

Riley sat at the back, with Miss Blandish lying on his feet, biting his nails.

James Hadley Chase, *No Orchids for Miss Blandish*

The dame walked close to me, and it was obvious that underneath her clothing she wore little or nothing.

Hank Janson, *Hotsy – You'll Be Chilled*

She had dark red hair and a fair skin which she told me came out in a mass of freckles at the first hint of sin.

Paul Mason, *City Without Justice*

I felt my hair being yanked cruelly as I tumbled to
the ground. Aubrey's hate-crazed face
hoovered over me.

Morton Cooper, *Confessions of a Striptease Artist*

From childhood to manhood, Julia and Harry lost no
time in engaging in amorous adventures.

Christopher Lewis, *Past Redemption*

Catherine had always been lucky. Even the sun was
shining when she first saw it.

Martin Hummerstone, 'Distant Horizons'

She would get new dresses, new bathing-costumes,
new everything. She would have a glorious bust.

Rachel Wing, 'Joy for Amanda'

On the floor above him lived a redheaded instructor in physical education, whose muscular calves he admired when they nodded to each other, by the mailbox.

E V Cunningham, *Sally*

He sat in the little flat in Chelsea blissfully eating crumpets over which Emily had spread the preposterous amount of butter which proceeds from an overflowing heart.

John Regardie, 'Story of Three Lives'

Slowly, almost one by one, Ordway's eyes followed the new steps in the snow.

Hammond Innes, *The White Tower*

The doctor smiled reassuringly at the worried mother and patted her little bot on the cheek.

Josephine Lawrence, *Prescription for Love*

She was a very neurotic woman with one leg in this world and the other in a world of her own. 'Between these two she doesn't know quite where she is,' said her solicitor.

Arthur Steward, 'The Circle of Mystery'

TWO

IT WAS A DARK AND STORMY NIGHT

Good Beginnings, Bad Beginnings and Even Worse Sex

Catching the reader's interest in books is difficult: what happens on that very first page can have a very big influence. Some writers have turned this into a fine art and others have always had a problem. Charles Dickens, for one, often struggled trying to get his story off the ground, which could seriously damage the potential of his work as it invariably first appeared in serial form. Indeed, he delivered one classic 'How Not to Do It' opening line for *Little Dorritt* (1855). 'Thirty years ago,' he wrote, 'Marseilles lay burning in the sun, one day.' He might have taken a leaf from the start of Franz Kafka's 'The Metamorphosis' – if the Czech author had been alive half a century earlier, of course – which begins, 'As Gregor Samsa awoke one morning from uneasy dreams, he found himself transformed in his bed into a gigantic insect.' Now that should make you want to read on!

In this chapter I have selected some of the best opening lines in literature. I have also included a number of other extracts from books that reveal the amusing and sometimes excruciating lengths authors have gone to in order to hold their readers' attention. Apart from these 'page turners' (on or off, the choice is there to be made), I have inserted some of the most hilarious sex scenes in popular fiction – an undertaking that has resulted in any number of pratfalls for the world's novelists. Among these selections are the winners of the 'Bad Sex Fiction Award' instituted in 1993 by Auberon Waugh, then editor of the *Literary Review*. This 'most dreaded literary honour' – to quote *The Times* – is given annually for the most crude, tasteless and often perfunctory 'bit of the other' in a novel. You have been warned!

The title of this chapter, incidentally, is taken from the opening paragraph of a notorious, rambling Victorian saga, *Paul Clifford*, which since 1982 has been the inspiration for another annual fiction competition run by San Jose State University for the 'worst opening sentence of the worst of all possible novels'.

It was a dark and stormy night, the rain fell in torrents – except at occasional intervals, when it was checked by a violent gust of wind which swept up the streets (for it is in London that our scene lies), rattling along the housetops and fiercely agitating the scanty flame of the lamps that struggled against the darkness.

Edward Bulwer-Lytton, *Paul Clifford* (1830)

A mistress should be like a little country retreat near the town; not to dwell in constantly, but only for a night and away!

William Wycherley, *The Country Wife* (1675)

Miss Bolo went straight home, in floods of tears and a sedan chair.

Charles Dickens, *Pickwick Papers* (1836)

She suddenly uttered a long and piercing shriek as he seized her. She appeared to be taken with an excess of delirium; she tore her hair, beat her bosom, used the most frantic gestures, and drawing a poniard from her girdle, plunged it into her.

Matthew Lewis, *The Monk* (1795)

It is a truth universally acknowledged that a single man in possession of a good fortune, must be in want of a wife.

Jane Austen, *Pride and Prejudice* (1813)

In the year 1775, there stood upon the borders of Epping Forest, at a distance of about twelve miles from London – measuring from the Standard in Cornhill or rather from the spot on or near to which the Standard used to be in days of yore – a house of public entertainment called The Maypole.

Charles Dickens, *Barnaby Rudge* (1841)

'Barbara! Barbara!' he ejaculated. 'I have seen Thorn!
Every drop of blood within me began to tingle, and
an impulse came upon me to spring upon him and
accuse him of the murder.'

Mrs Henry Wood, *East Lynne* (1861)

One thing was certain, that was the white kitten had
had nothing to do with it – it was the black kitten's
fault entirely.

Lewis Carroll, *Through the Looking-Glass* (1872)

I am nothing to you. I know I never touched a fibre
of your heart or fancy. But better would it be for you
to love a man dead in a coffin, than to love one to
whom at any hour the law may snatch from you and
send to fret his years away in the horrors of prison.

Ouida (Louise Ramé), *In Maremma* (1882)

Buck did not read the newspapers or he would have known that trouble was brewing, not alone for himself, but for every tidewater dog, strong of muscle and with warm, long hair, from Puget Sound to San Diego.

Jack London, *Call of the Wild* (1903)

The human race, to which so many of my readers belong...

G K Chesterton, *The Napoleon of Notting Hill* (1904)

Once upon a time and a very good time it was there was a moocow coming down along the road and this moocow that was coming down along the road met a nicens little boy named baby tuckoo.

James Joyce, *Portrait of the Artist as a Young Man* (1917)

Henry Lakington is the second most
dangerous man in London.

'Sapper' (Herman Cyril Mcneile),
Bull-Dog Drummond (1920)

His body vibrated taut and powerful as he closed
upon her and crushed her, breathless and dazed and
destroyed, crushed her upon his breast. Ah, it was
terrible and perfect.

D H Lawrence, *Women in Love* (1920)

I believe that a well-known anecdote exists to the
effect that a young writer, determined to make the
commencement of his story forcible and original
enough to catch and rivet the attention of the most
blasé of editors, penned the following sentence:
'Hell!' said the Duchess.'

Agatha Christie, *The Murder on the Links* (1923)

'Sent down for indecent behaviour, eh?' said Paul
Pennyfeather's guardian.

Evelyn Waugh, *Decline and Fall* (1928)

Some things can't be ravished. You can't ravish a tin
of sardines.

D H Lawrence, *Lady Chatterley's Lover* (1928)

He spent his declining years trying
to guess the answer to the Irish question.
Unfortunately, whenever he was getting warm, the
Irish secretly changed
the question.

W C Sellar & R J Yeatman, *1066 And All That* (1930)

'Damn, I'm late,' Bernard said to himself as he first
caught sight of Big Henry, the Singery clock.

Aldous Huxley, *Brave New World* (1932)

Names and descriptions of Broadcasting House have
varied from the complimentary to the scurrilous. It
has been called [everything from] a worthy edifice
well fitted to the marvels it contains to a damned
awful erection.

Val Gielgud, *Death at Broadcasting House* (1934)

Hale knew, before he had been in
Brighton three hours, that they meant
to murder him.

Graham Greene, *Brighton Rock* (1938)

I am a camera with its shutter open, quite passive,
recording, not thinking.

Christopher Isherwood, *Goodbye to Berlin* (1939)

Gee! Only one woman a year, and that a dead 'un!

Jonathan Latimer, *Naboth's Vineyard* (1943)

When Mrs Frederick C Little's second son arrived, everybody noticed that he was not much bigger than a mouse.

E H White, *Stuart Little* (1945)

Bang! Bang! Bang! Three shots in the groin and I was off on the greatest adventure of my life.

Thomas Kingston, *Sleep Till Noon* (1946)

I guess I'm just an old mad scientist at bottom. Give me an underground laboratory, half a dozen atom smashers, and a beautiful girl in a diaphanous veil waiting to be turned into a chimpanzee, and I care not who writes the nation's laws.

S J Perelman, *One Touch of Venus* (1948)

It was a bright cold day in April and the clocks were striking thirteen.

George Orwell, *Nineteen Eighty-Four* (1949)

If you really want to hear about it, the first thing you'll probably want to know is where I was born, and what my lousy childhood was like, and how my parents were occupied and all before they had me, and all of that David Copperfield kind of crap.

J D Salinger, *The Catcher in the Rye* (1951)

I write this sitting in the kitchen sink.

Dodie Smith, *I Capture the Castle* (1952)

The past is a foreign country: they do things differently there.

L P Hartley, *The Go-Between* (1953)

The scene and smoke and sweat of a casino are nauseating at three in the morning.

Ian Fleming, *Casino Royale* (1953)

'There's such a thing as the Chastity
of Women Act, which prevents one speaking out.
And I've no wish to take away another's character,
even if she does move in high society where those
things don't matter.

Honor Tracy, *The Deserters* (1954)

Lolita, light of my life, fire of my loins,
my sin, my soul.

Vladimir Nabokov, *Lolita* (1955)

Wynstan's arms tightened as she spoke.
'I am not . . . really sure . . . about what men and
women . . . do when they . . . make love . . . but it
must be . . . wonderful . . .'

Barbara Cartland, *No Time For Love* (1956)

Nothing happens, nobody comes, nobody goes.
It's awful.

Samuel Beckett, *Waiting for Godot* (1956)

They're out there.

Ken Kesey, *One Flew Over the Cuckoo's Nest* (1960)

David arrived at Coetminais the afternoon after
the one he had landed at Cherbourg and driven
down to Avarnaches, where he had spent the
intervening Tuesday night.

John Fowles, *The Collector* (1963)

I'm going to get that bloody bastard
if I die in the attempt.

James Clavell, *King Rat* (1965)

Many years later, as he faced the firing
squad, Colonel Aureliano Buendia was to remember
that distant afternoon when his father took him
to discover ice.

Gabriel García Marquéz, *One Hundred Years of
Solitude* (1967)

It was love at first sight.

Joseph Heller, *Catch 22* (1968)

———

What can you say about a twenty-five-year-old girl who died?

Eric Segal, *Love Story* (1968)

———

It all began so suddenly. The reptilian forces of Megenth, long quiescent, suddenly began to expand due to the serum given them by Charles Engstrom, the power-crazed telepath.

Robert Sheckley, *Zirn Left Unguarded* (1969)

———

Death was a grim business in the Middle Ages.

Thomas Boase, *Death in the Middle Ages* (1972)

———

There were 117 psychoanalysts on the Pan Am flight to Vienna and I'd been treated by at least six of them.

Erica Jong, *Fear of Flying* (1973)

I can see by my watch, without taking my hand from the left grip of the cycle, that it is eight-thirty in the morning.

Robert M Pirsig, *Zen and the Art of Motorcycle Maintenance* (1974)

I want a sense of purpose in my life.
I don't want to die in Chelsea with
my knickers down.

Jilly Cooper, *Emily* (1975)

Even before the deal with Straker had been
consummated (that's some word all right, he
thought, and his eyes crawled over the front of his
secretary's blouse), Lawrence Crockett was, without
doubt, the richest man in Salem's Lot and one of the
richest in Cumberland County, although there
was nothing about his office or his
person to indicate it.

Stephen King, *Salem's Lot* (1975)

One of the things Ford Prefect had always found
hardest to understand about human beings was their
habit of continually stating or repeating the obvious,
as in 'it's a nice day,' or 'you're very tall,' or 'oh,
dear, you seem to have fallen down a 30ft well.'

Douglas Adams, *The Hitchhiker's Guide to the Galaxy*
(1979)

It was the afternoon of my eighty-first birthday, and
I was in bed with my catamite when Ali announced
that the archbishop had come to see me.

Anthony Burgess, *Earthly Powers* (1980)

As they lay together, half asleep, but unwilling to drift apart into unconsciousness, Daisy farted, in a tiny series of absolutely irrepressible little pops that seemed to her to go on for a minute.

Judith Krantz, *Princess Daisy* (1980)

The blood that had abandoned her countenance rushed into his.

Elizabeth Peters, *The Lion in the Valley* (1986)

I intensely disliked my father's fifth wife, but not to the point of murder.

Dick Francis, *Hot Money* (1987)

She wanted to wrap her legs around him the way a tree wraps itself around a mountain.

Jan Stacy, *Bodysmasher* (1988)

By the end of the alley, the fine hairs in my nostrils were starting to twitch.

Lindsay Davis, *Shadows in Bronze* (1990)

She wore a dress the same colour as her eyes her father brought her from San Francisco.

Danielle Steel, *Star* (1993)

Their jaws ground in feverish mutual mastication. Saliva and sweat. Sweat and saliva. There was a purposeful shedding of clothes.

Philip Hook, *The Stonebreakers* (1994)

His tremulous thumbs gathered the elastic waist of her panties and plucked them down over the twin golden domes of her behind and back up the suspended sentences and Sobranie filtered tips of her stocking tops. Detached mind from over-eager gnomen and its exquisitely appointed, shadowy task, he began to make love to her. When they had finished they lay under the sheet and watched TV.

Philip Kerr, *Gridiron* (1995)

As Jean-Claude explored her body with his own, teased and titillated her with his lips and tongue, she felt an explosion of such intensity that it made her body shake. She also felt an enormous outpouring of love. She had pretended for years that she didn't need it, or want it. And so it began.

Joan Collins, *Too Damn Famous* (1995)

He was as guarded as a virgin,
but infinitely more experienced.

Cathy Spellman, *An Excess of Love* (1996)

Eighteen years ago on the night of her eighth birthday, in a seaside cottage on Key West, Chyna had squirmed under her bed to hide from Jim Woltz, her mother's friend. A storm had been raging from the Gulf of Mexico, and the sky-blistering lightning had made her fearful of escaping the sanctuary of the beach where she'd retreated on other nights. After committing herself to the cramped space under the iron bed, which had been lower slung than this one, she had discovered that she was sharing it with a palmetto beetle.

Dean Koontz, *Intensity* (1996)

—⋅—

'Stick it in,' she whispered. I moved up the bed and pushed inside her. Liz squeaked like wet rubber. She grabbed my love handles and ground her hips against me, her eyes like black saucers, staring into mine as she hooked a yoga-leg onto my shoulder. We went through a medley of our favourite positions.

David Huggins, *The Big Kiss* (1996)

—⋅—

I remember the first time I travelled on Concorde.
I was totally in awe of the number of internationally
famous faces on board and it was some time before
I noticed the passengers were in fact casting
surreptitious glances at me. It was then that it
dawned on me that mine was the most famous face
of all.

Naomi Campbell, *Swan* (1996)

We were making out all the way up her stairs; as we
got inside her apartment, we just started screwing.
She stopped me, got up naked and walked to the
bathroom and started to vomit.

Ethan Hawke, *The Hottest State* (1997)

Yasmin grinned and writhed on the bed, arching
her back, making a noise somewhere between
a beached seal and a police siren.

Nicholas Royle, *The Matter of the Heart* (1997)

The knife was poised above her heart. Her screams cut through the dead, rotten air of the warehouse. Batiste Legendre smiled. He bent down and soul-kissed the terrified eighteen-year-old who was to remain that age forever.

Vincent Courtney, *Vampire Beat* (1998)

His hands stroked her shoulders and arms, then slid the Lycra top off her waist revealing her perfectly formed breasts. By the time they had slipped naked under the duvet he was lost in the warmth and fragrant passion of Lisa Drake.

Alan Titchmarsh, *Mr MacGregor* (1998)

Meanwhile her ears were filled with the sound of a soft but frantic gasping and it was some time before she identified it as her own.

Sebastian Faulks, *Charlotte Gray* (1998)

The rash-rubbed thighs clamped cheeks, bits
of liverish flesh draped across his nose and coarse
hair scraped his chin. There seemed to be such a
lot of her.

A A Gill, *Starcrossed* (1999)

—•—

All was chaos. In the universe of James T Kirk his
bride lay dying, their unborn child within her. In
the plasma storms of the Badlands, three starships
held an impossible portal open to another reality.

William Shatner, *Star Trek: Preserver* (2000)

—•—

Her small white body. She is so small and compact,
and yet she has all the necessary features. Shall I
compare thee to a Sony Walkman, thou art more
compact and more. She is his own Toshiba, his dinky
little JVC, his sweet Aiwa.

Sean Thomas, *Kissing England* (2000)

—•—

He brings his body up next to hers. Mirabelle, foetal, curled up like a bug, receives the proximity of Ray Porter as though it were a nourishing stream. They wake in the morning on either side of the bed.

Steve Martin, *Shopgirl* (2000)

Her hand is moving away from my knee and heading north. Heading unnervingly and with a steely will towards the pole. And like Sir Ranulph Fiennes, Pamela will not easily be discouraged.

Christopher Hart, *Rescue Me* (2001)

Professor Malik Solanka, retired historian of ideas, irascible dollmaker, and since his recent fifty-fifth birthday, celibate and solitary by his own (much criticized) choice, in his silvered years found himself living in a golden age.

Salman Rushdie, *Fury* (2001)

And then he was fully socketed to her, like a pipe
wrench in a crock of warm chilli.

Robert Tanenbaum, *Act of Revenge* (2001)

She felt herself aching with the furtive control she
had taken over him. If she were to take some
pleasure of him while he slept, he need never know.

Sebastian Faulks, *On Green Dolphin Street* (2001)

I was 21 years old, queer and a Buckingham Palace
footman in 1967 when, for the first time, I found
myself drawn to a political figure who was neither
Lady Violet Bonham-Carter or Bessie Braddock.

Guy Hunting, *Adventures of a Gentleman's Gentleman*
(2002)

She popped the elastic at the top of the second sock
and pushed her sexually ambiguous Timex watch up
along the blond hairs of her handsome forearms.

Steve Whalen, *A Love Story* (2002)

His head has been pushed down into the dusty bedclothes, so he cannot see the purple face of the man toiling behind him. He is aware, however, that the pounding is punctuated by buttock-slaps and regular full-throated hunting cries as the major's excitement mounts. 'Tally-ho!' gives way to 'On! On! On!' and the bed groans with the effort of maintaining its structural integrity.

Hari Kunzru, *The Impressionist* (2002)

She closed her eyes, saw his dark-as-treacle-toffee eyes gazing down at her. Weirdly, he was clad in pinstripes at the same time as being naked. Pinstripes were erotic, the uniform of fathers, two-dimensional fathers. Even his penis had a seductive pinstriped foreskin.

Wendy Perrian, *Tread Softly* (2002)

When he finally came, it was like dropping a naked electric cable into a fish tank.

Nicholas Blincoe, *White Mice* (2002)

Deidra had quite phenomenal nipples. They were huge and dark brown, and when aroused startlingly erect. Men flipped over her nipples.

Jackie Collins, *Hollywood Wives – The New Generation* (2003)

She is topping up your engine oil for the cross-country coming up. Your RPM is hitting a new high. To wait any longer would be to lose prime time. She picks up a Bugatti's momentum. You want her more at a Volkswagen's steady trot. Squeeze the maximum mileage out of your gallon of gas. But she's eating up the road with all cylinders blazing.

Aniruddha Bahalm, *Bunker 13* (2003)

Many last lines of books are also memorable in the same kind of absurd or humorous way as those above. As a taster, here are two classics. The first is from Percy Shelley's *The Cenci*, which closes with, 'And yours, I see, is coming down'; and the second from Terry Southern and Mason Hoffenburg's *Candy*, with the heroine's startled exclamation, 'Good grief – it's Daddy!'

THREE

Amorous Propensities

A Risqué Choice of Double Entendres

Double entendres, whether intentional or not, can be the bane of any writer's life, though this is none more true than in the world of book publishing, where any typo, mistake or double entendre can potentially live forever.

The author Sir John Betjeman once gave a talk that I covered for my newspaper and during this told an amusing story about a little boy – himself possibly? – who was fascinated by his grandmother's ability to get wild birds to feed on her windowsill. A pair of bluetits were so tame that they would take crumbs from her hand. One particular day, said Betjeman with a smile, the boy ran into a room where his parents were entertaining some guests and shrieked with delight, 'Mummy, Daddy, I've just seen Grandma's tits.' Another popular speaker of the era, Chips Channon, delighted audiences with stories of his love for the novels of Anthony Trollope. 'There's nothing I like better,' he would grin mischievously, 'than lying on my bed for an hour or so with my favourite Trollope.'

So without further ado, here is a selection of the ripest double entendres that I have been able to cull from the pages of our finest authors – a selection where such familiar favourites as Jane Austen, Charles Dickens and Henry James will unwittingly be found among the worst culprits...

He wants to visit with the head of his hanging
piece the familiar hole he has often filled before
with its equal length.

Anonymous, *The Key* (c fourteenth century)

I felt, me thought, two fiery balls fly whizzing
through my liver,
And Beauty, a bold thief, cried
'Stand – Deliver!'

Giovanni Guarini, *The Pastor Fido* (1585)

How brave a prospect is a bright back-side!

Henry Vaughan, Thalia Rediviva: *The Pastimes &
Diversions of a Country Muse* (1678)

The confidence which presumes to do, by surveying
the surface, what labour only can perform, by
penetrating the bottom.

Samuel Johnson, *The Rambler* (1748)

Soon after came the Prince of Wales and Prince Edward; and then the Lady Augusta, all quite undressed, and they took their stools and sat round the fire with us.

George Dodington, *Journal* (1754)

I won't go about to argue the point with you – 'tis so – and I am persuaded of it, madam, as much as can be, 'That both man and woman bear pain or sorrow (and, for aught I know, pleasure too) best in a horizontal position.'

Laurence Sterne, *The Life and Opinions of Tristram Shandy* (1759)

I'll come no more behind your scenes, David, for the silk stockings and white bosoms of your actresses excite my amorous propensities.

James Boswell, *Life of Samuel Johnson* (1791)

Soon shalt thou hear the bridegroom's voice, The
midnight cry, 'Behold, I come!'

James Lowes, *The Midnight Cry* (1800)

I dined at Deane yesterday and met the two Mr
Holders. We played at Vingt-un, which as Fulwar was
unsuccessful, gave him an opportunity of exposing
himself as usual.

Jane Austen, *Letters to Cassandra* (1801)

In winter, his private balls were numerous enough
for any young lady who was not suffering under the
insatiable appetite of fifteen.

Jane Austen, *Sense and Sensibility* (1811)

On entering the drawing-room, she found the whole
party at loo and was immediately invited
to join them.

Jane Austen, *Pride and Prejudice* (1813)

Mrs Goddard was the mistress of a school – not of a seminary, or an establishment, or anything which professed, in long sentences of refined nonsense to combine liberal acquirements with elegant morality upon new principles and new systems – and where young ladies for enormous pay might be screwed out of health and into vanity.

Jane Austen, *Emma* (1816)

Such was Catherine Morland at ten. At fifteen appearances were mending; she began to cut her hair and long for balls.

Jane Austen, *Northanger Abbey* (1818)

From my window I saw them running through the garden in every direction, embracing each other, ejaculating, playing, and counting their beads, with hands tremulous and eyes uplifted in ecstasy.

Charles Robert Maturin, *Melmoth the Wanderer* (1820)

She touched the organ;
I could stand for hours and hours.

Winthrop Praed, *The Belle of the Ballroom* (1828)

Sebald, as we lay,
Rising and falling only with our pants, Who said,
'Let Death come now – 'tis right to die!'

Robert Browning, *Pippa Passes* (1841)

She touched his organ, and from that bright epoch,
even it, the old companion of his happiest hours,
incapable as he had thought of elevation, began a
new and deified existence.

Charles Dickens, *Martin Chuzzlewit* (1843)

I deeply appreciate his talent for the organ,
notwithstanding that I do not, if I may use the
expression, grind myself.

Charles Dickens, *Martin Chuzzlewit* (1843)

'My master,' he says, 'has forewarned me. Daily he announces more distinctly, "Surely I come quickly" and hourly I more eagerly respond, "Amen! Even so, come, Lord Jesus!"'

Charlotte Brontë, *Jane Eyre* (1847)

———

Miss Sedley's new femme de chambre refused to go to bed without a wax candle.

William Makepeace Thackeray, *Vanity Fair* (1847–8)

———

The organ begins to swell;
She's coming, she's coming!
My lady comes at last.

William Makepeace Thackeray,
At the Church Gate (1854)

———

He had a spectacle case in his hand, which he turned over and over while he was thus in question, with a certain free use of the thumb which is never seen but in a hand accustomed to tools.

Charles Dickens, *Little Dorrit* (1855–7)

No public business of any kind could possibly be
done at any time without the acquiescence of the
Circumlocution Office. Its finger was in the largest
public pie and in the smallest public tart.

Charles Dickens, *Little Dorrit* (1855–7)

He flourished his tool. The end of the lash just
touched my forehead. A warm, excited thrill ran
through my veins, my blood seemed to give a bound,
and then raced fast and hot along its channels. I got
up nimbly, came round to where he stood,
and faced him.

Charlotte Brontë, *The Professor* (1857)

And when you had found him, you found a man
superficially coy perhaps, but at bottom always
ready to do business.

Charles Reade, *It's Never Too Late to Mend* (1856)

What'er is done in this sweet isle,
There's none that may not lift his horn,
If only lifted with a smile.

William Johnson Cory, *Ionica*, Poems (1858)

A boy's sheepishness is by no means a sign of over-mastering reverence; and while you are making encouraging advances to him under the idea that he is overwhelmed by a sense of your age and wisdom, ten to one he is thinking you extremely queer.

George Eliot (Mary Ann Evans),
The Mill on the Floss (1860)

Mrs Glegg had doubtless the glossiest and crispest brown curls in her drawers, as well as curls in various degrees of fuzzy laxness.

George Eliot, *The Mill on the Floss* (1860)

I had cherished a profound conviction that her bringing me up by hand gave her no right to bring me up by jerks.

Charles Dickens, *Great Expectations* (1860–61)

Mrs Ray declared that she had not found it at all hard and then – with laudable curiosity, seeing how little she had known about balls – desired to have an immediate account of Rachel's doings.

Anthony Trollope, *Rachel Ray* (1861)

He had an unbounded enthusiasm for French letters. He lost his sense of proportion in that matter.

George Meredith, *Modern Love* (1862)

I am not going to offer – still less urge – marriage now. But I insist on free intercourse – face to face.

John Ruskin, *Sesame and Lilies* (1864–9)

I like my balls very well and have
also received the money.

William Hazlitt, *Memoirs* (1867)

A young Irish girl, going from Albany to New York
to a situation, lost her written recommendation.
Having an old friend in the city, she appealed to him
to help her. The following is a copy of his certificate:
'This is to certify that Bridget Mahony had a good
character when she left Albany, but lost it on the
steamboat going down.'

Anonymous, *The Book of Blunders* (1871)

As big as any man could wish to have,
and lined inside, and doubled-lined in the lower
parts, and extra piece of stiffening
at the bottom.

Thomas Hardy, *Under The Greenwood Tree* (1872)

Never travel a long journey without having your
drawers lined smoothly and carefully with chamois
leather or buckskin.

John Spencer, *Bicycling – A Book for Early Riders*
(1874)

'Oh, I can't explain!' cried Roderick impatiently,
returning to his work. 'I've only one way of
expressing my deepest feelings – it's this.' And he
swung his tool.

Henry James, *Roderick Hudson* (1875)

'This here's a Bramah pick-lock, sir,' says Critchett,
displaying an elegant little tool.

Ouida (Louise Ramé), *An Altruist* (1875)

'You think me a queer fellow already.
It's not easy, either, to tell you what I feel. Not easy
at all for so queer a fellow as I tell you in how many
ways he's queer.'

Henry James, *A Passionate Pilgrim* (1875)

No woman was happier in her choice – no woman –
and after two months of uninterrupted intercourse,
there is still more cause for thankfulness.

Elizabeth Barrett Browning, *Letters* (1876)

'It's just like Longueville, you know,' Gordon Wright
went on; 'he always comes at you from behind; he's
so awfully fond of surprises.'

Henry James, *Confidence* (1880)

She gave a little scream and a jerk, and so relieved
herself.

Anthony Trollope, *The Duke's Children* (1880)

She realised at last that she had no vocation for
struggling with her combinations.

Henry James, *The Portrait of a Lady* (1881)

Gradually, when he found his sensitive organ grateful even for grim favours, he conferred them with a lighter hand.

Henry James, *The Portrait of a Lady* (1881)

'Well, now, you look here, that was a good lay of yours last night. I don't deny it was a good lay. Some of you pretty handy with a hand-spike end.'

Robert Louis Stevenson, *Treasure Island* (1883)

Prince of the school, he had gained an easy domination over the old Greek master by the fascination of his parts.

Walter Pater, *Marius the Epicurean* (1885)

What he heard was the tear of the ripping tool as it ploughed its way along the sticky parting.

Thomas Hardy, *The Woodlanders* (1887)

'My boy!' he said – and, if you'll believe it, his very voice was queer, almost shaky and a little broken and hoarse, not at all what you would expect an earl's voice to be, though he spoke more decidedly and peremptorily even than before – 'yes, you'll be my boy as long as I live; and, by George, sometimes I feel as if you were the only boy I ever had.'

Frances Hodgson Burnett, *Little Lord Fauntleroy* (1886)

Now the time was coming when I began to think about helping the princes by fetching their balls up from the bottom.

John Ruskin, *Praeterita* (1886-8)

It was the constant theme of his French friends. They believed that at bottom he was sorer than they were. They, however, were perpetually in the breach.

Henry James, *The Princess Casamassima* (1886)

This time I left the excuses to his more practised
patience, only relieving myself in response to a
direct appeal from a young lady with whom, in the
hall, I found myself sitting.

Henry James, *The Reverberator* (1888)

The only thing I can think about now is being hard
up. I suppose having my hands in my pockets has
made me think of this.

Jerome K Jerome, *The Idle Thoughts of an Idle Fellow*
(1889)

Mr Longdon, resisting, kept erect with a low gasp
that his host only was near enough to catch. This
suddenly appeared to confirm an impression
gathered by Vanderbank in their contact, a strange
sense that his visitor was so agitated as
to be trembling in every limb. It brought to his lips a
kind of ejaculation.

Henry James, *The Awkward Age* (1899)

What an intimacy, what an intensity of relation, I said to myself, so successful a process implied! It was, of course, familiar enough that when people were so deeply in love they rubbed off on each other.

Henry James, *The Sacred Fount* (1900)

Then she had had her equal consciousness that, within five minutes, something between them had – well, she couldn't call it anything but come.

Henry James, *The Wings of the Dove* (1902)

I had done Miss Churm at the piano before.

Henry James, *The Real Thing* (1903)

I was nearly a man now; I would be afraid of things no more; I would get out my pendulum and see whether that would not help me. The pendulum should wag and have a fair chance of doing its best.

George MacDonald, *Wilfred Cumbermede* (1904)

'Stop a minute; let those two people go on, or I shall have to speak to them. I do detest conventional intercourse. Nasty! They are going into the church, too. Oh, the Britisher abroad!'

E M Forster, *A Room with a View* (1908)

Next after that slow-coming, slow-going smile of her lover, it was the rusty complexion of his patrimonial marbles that she most prized.

Henry James, *The Last of the Valerii* (1909)

Go, spend your penny, Beauty, when you will, In the grave's darkness let the stamp be lost. The water still will bubble.

John Masefield, *Lollingdon Downs* (1910)

He reached his room to find three other boys busily engaged in abusing their housemaster.

Horace Annesley Vachell, *The Hill* (1914)

'Well!' said the Duchess to me, 'apart from your
balls, can't I be of any use to you?'

Marcel Proust, *Cities of the Plain* (1921)

———

And when you'd a mind to career
Off anywhere – say to town –
You were all of a sudden gone
Before I had thought thereon,
Or noticed your trunks were down.

Thomas Hardy, *Without Ceremony* (1922)

———

Having for years had no real
intercourse with any one save his wife,
he was very shy.

Dame Ethel Smyth, *Impressions that Remain* (1922)

———

Country ladies are not like London ones, who can
take a dinner, an opera, two balls and an at-home in
one and the same night.

Robert Surtees, *Ask Mamma* (1924)

Eustace came too and knelt quietly enough between
his aunts. But when it was over he at once got up and
began hunting for something.
'Why! Someone has cut my whistle
in two,' he said.

E M Forster, *The Story of a Panic* (1928)

⎯⎯•⎯⎯

'Hang your theories!' said Parker. 'It looks to me as if
we shall have to wash out the idea that General
Fentiman got his dose in Portman Square.'

Dorothy L Sayers
The Unpleasantness at the Bellona Club (1928)

⎯⎯•⎯⎯

Here is a wonderful and delightful thing, that we
should have furnished ourselves with orifices, with
traps that open and shut, through which to push and
pour alien objects that give us such pleasurable, such
delicious sensations.

Rose Macaulay, *Personal Pleasures* (1935)

⎯⎯•⎯⎯

What is more beautiful for the blonde to wear for formal dances than white tulle? My answer – and I'm sure you will agree with me – is 'Nothing'.

Barbara Cartland, *Etiquette* (1952)

Mind you, I never made advances to a woman who wouldn't have gladly acknowledged to thirty-five. And I gave them love. Why, many of them had never known what it was to have a man do them up behind.

W Somerset Maugham, *The Round Dozen* (1953)

Mr Grant, really quite glad of an excuse to dismount, offered his cock to Lydia, who immediately flung a leg over it, explaining that she had put on a frock with pleats on purpose.

Angela Thirkell, *The Brandons* (1953)

But I remember more dearly autumn afternoons in bottoms that lay intensely silent under old and great trees.

C S Lewis, *Surprised by Joy* (1955)

The chief purpose of Mrs Roosevelt in coming to London was to have intercourse with the American troops.

Gilbert Harding, *Along My Line* (1956)

'I should like balls infinitely better,' said Caroline Bingley, 'if they were carried in a different manner.'

C S Lewis, *Undeceptions* (1971)

She continued to argue for the truth until gunpowder and faggots consumed her.

Pauline Nadir, *The King's Ladies* (2000)

FOUR

SODS I HAVE CUT ON THE TURF

A Library of Weird Titles

Book titles are vital to get right, especially for the author and the publisher. For the reader, browsing the bookshop shelves, the title of any book has to be eye-catching *and* informative – and sometimes for the author and publisher this can be a task that brings a challenge full of compromise…and hilarity.

This next chapter contains a handful of the titles (plus their subtitles thrown in for good measure!) from among the hundreds that I discovered during publishing trips to America and Europe as well as from research in the British Library, the New York Public Library and the Library of Congress in Washington, DC, not forgetting the libraries of other book collectors. Here, then, is my collection of weird and wonderful books – many of them with titles almost too bad to be true, but with a guarantee that every one is absolutely genuine…

Benefits of Farting Explained
Don Fartando
(Fleet Street, 1602)

A translation from the Spanish by Obidah Fizle.'

———

A Big Cock and a Leaking Mouth, Cheng Hsie
(Shanghai publishing Co, 1964)

'It is a bad habit for children to have a meal walking
about and dropping rice.'

The Big Problem of Small Organs
Alan T Kitley (Privately published, 1966)

'The results of ten years devising schemes for
small organs.'

Blondes Prefer Gentlemen, 'Melita Noose' (Stanley
Paul, 1926)

'Every girl is mistress of her own fate and can get on
it if she wants to.'

Blondie Beg Your Bullet, Rick Razio
(MC Publications, 1957)

'The man who makes the gangsters quake and the
women quiver.'

Bowels Opened, Reverend Sibbes & Katherine Hall
(Cambridge, 1642)

'A discovery of the near and dear love.'

———•———

Briefs Calmly Considered, Thomas Taylor
(Anthony Berkley, 1826)

'A layman's guide to the passage of the law.'

———•———

Brooklyn Moll Shoots Bedmate
Ernest McKeag (Modern Fiction, 1951)

'The scandal sheets all wanted to cover this gal.'

———•———

Camping Among Cannibals,
Alfred St Johnston (Macmillan, 1883)

'The exploits of an explorer among savages
who eat human flesh.'

———•———

Confessions of a Groper, Samu Yamamoto (Chikan
Press, 1997)

'Gradually you discover the most amazing thing
— no one stops you.'

———

Couplings up the Khyber, Percy Berridge (David &
Charles, 1969)

'Railway stories from a far-flung corner.'

———

Crick Bottom, Ellsworthy Conkle
(Samuel French, 1928)

'Another lively entertainment about a
small country seat.'

———

Cult of the Clitoris, Noel Pemberton-Billing (Vigilante
Publishing Co, 1918)

'An exaggerated clitoris might drive a woman to a
bull elephant.'

———

Dames Fry Too, Dick Hudsen
(Gannet Press Ltd, 1954)

'Things would only get hotter when she tangled
with the Private Dick.'

Dumps, Mrs E T Meade (Chambers, 1905)

'The story of a plain girl and her struggles in life.'

Dykes on Bikes, Alan Marshall
(Lion Books, 1973)

'There was no hell on earth like these girls!'

Every Frenchman Has One
Olivia De Havilland (Paul Elek, 1963)

'The intimate revelations of a great
Hollywood film star.'

Fables of Abundance, Jackson Lears (Hollywood House, 1974)

'The dream of glimpsing half-dressed women unawares.'

Farting Candles, Lillian Sayce (Skeffington, 1935)

'A masterpiece of pungent brevity about the scandalous ladies of Upwitham.'

Fifty Years with the Rod, John Stirling (Philip Allan, 1929)

'A lifetime of great catches by the President of the Scottish Anglers' Association.'

Fountain of Youth, Dr Benedict Lust (Macfadden Publications, 1923)

'Contains full details of Dr Lust's Technique of Rectal Irrigation.'

Franny Dill, Woodrow Olivetti
(Triumph Books, 1967)

'The scorching saga of a teenage sex-bomb.'

The Future of Nakedness, John Langdon-Davies (Noel
Douglas, 1929)

'A revealing look at where our obsession with
clothes is leading.'

Gay Boys of Old Yale, John Denison Vose (Hunter
Books, 1869)

'Carefree varsity days recalled by one of them.'

Gay Crusaders, Magdalen King-Hall
(Peter Davis, 1934)

'A stirring romance of men of action in
the Middle Ages.'

Glad to be Bad, Adam Roberts
(Midwood, 1977)

'Gorgeous Gwen was always willing to give a
little to get a lot.'

———

Grand Opening, Alice Leeds
(Thomas Nelson, 1980)

'A year in the life of a total wife.'

———

Green Balls, Paul Bewsher
(Blackwood & Sons, 1919)

'The dramatic adventures of a Night Bomber.'

———

Groping, Naomi Jacob (Hutchinson, 1933)

'The intimate story of Marcus Stern's struggle
against adversity.'

———

Half-Cocked, Violet Grey
(Command Books, 1975)

'He was hard up and horny all the time but
only half a man.'

———

Her Candle Burns Hot, Hodge Evans (Rainbow Books,
1970)

'On her wedding night a strange man walked in . . .'

———

History of Fanny Thoughtless, Anonymous (J Davis,
1825)

'What befell naughty Fanny when she would not
learn her lesson.'

———

Hookers of Kew, Mea Allan
(Michael Joseph, 1967)

'A revealing biography of the eminent family of
botanists.'

———

How to Avoid Intercourse with your Unfriendly Car Mechanic, Harold M Landy (Ashley Books, 1977)

'A guide to getting the best servicing.'

———

Invisible Dick, Frank Topham
(D C Thompson, 1936)

'"What a disgraceful scene," said Dick Brett, doing a series of physical jerks behind a bush.'

———

Joyful Lays, Richard Lowry & Howard Doane (Biglow & Main, 1886)

'Words and music for rousing passion in worship.'

———

Leadership Secrets of Attila the Hun,
Wess Roberts (Bantam Press, 1989)

'Good Huns normally achieve what their chieftain expects of them.'

———

Lesbia's Little Blunder, Bessie Marchant
(Frederick Warne, 1934)

'Lesbia has to learn that love wins the affection
of her school chums.'

Living with Crazy Buttocks, Kaz Cooke (Penguin,
2002)

'Another comic milestone by the author of *Real
Gorgeous*.'

Love Slave of the Scientists,
Frank Belknap Long (Avon Books, 1953)

'When the scientists invented these delectable toys
they reckoned without the unstable passions of wives.'

Love Sonnets of a Hoodlum, Wallace Irwin
(Paul Elder & Co, 1901)

'The vagaries of a man of the world.'

Loves of a Girl Wrestler, Ben West
(Beacon Books, 1969)

'A Terror in the Ring...A Tigress in the Boudoir.'

Making It in Leather, Vincent Hayes
(Drake Publishers, 1972)

'The secrets of beautiful designs for family
and friends.'

A Man, a Maid and Saturn's Temptation, Stanley G
Weinbaum (Avon Books, 1953)

'Diana Vick had his jealously sought jewels in her
hand and a morass ahead.'

Memorable Balls, James Laver
(Derek Verschoyle, 1954)

'An eminent historian's study of some great social
entertainments.'

Naked on Roller Skates, Maxwell Bodenheim
(Monarch Books, 1954)

'Bump and grind was their idea of fun.'

Nautipuss, Clyde Allison
(Ember Library, 1985)

'Agent 0008 Battles the Temptress of the Deep.'

Penetrating Wagner's Ring, John Di Gaetanao (De
Capo Press, 1978)

'A musician's in-depth examination of the great
composer's most famous creation.'

Perfect 36, Ed Springarn
(Pyramid Books, 1973)

'A revealing story of the bosom business.'

Perverse Pussy, Anonymous
(American Sunday-School Union, 1869)

'The story of raising a difficult cat – and the
lessons to be drawn.'

—•—

Pit Stop Nympho, Peter Kevin
(Imperial Books, 1978)

'Into the high tension world of Grand Prix racing
roars red-hot lust!'

—•—

Planet of the Knob Heads, Stanton A Coblentz (Blue
Ribbon, 1939)

'It was a race against time to save the women from
their deadly embrace.'

—•—

Queer Shipmates, Archibald Campbell
(Phoenix House, 1962)

'Afloat on the oceans of the world with some
unusual seamen.'

Queer Sisters, Steve Harragani
(Stallion Books, 1963)

'A penetrating story of Society's Greatest Curse:
Homosexuality!'

———

Quickie! Gerald Foster
(Quarter Books, 1974)

'She was always one jump ahead of the mobsters.'

———

Resistance of Piles to Penetration,
Russell V Allin (Spon, 1935)

'Essential study for all those engaged in
the building industry.'

———

Romantic Shorts, Mollie Panter-Downes
(Swan, 1941)

'Audrey was left breathless by the fervour
of his love-making.'

———

Saddle of Queens, Louise Bloodgood
(J A Allen, 1959)

'Some of the great historical rides of royalty.'

Sauciest Boy in the Service, W Gordon Stables
(Ward Lock, 1905)

'A story of pluck and perseverance among
staunch military men.'

Scouts in Bondage, Geoffrey Prout
(Aldine Publishing Co, 1930)

'Helpful hints for Boy Scouts to lead more
adventurous lives.'

She Vamped A Strangler, Henri Duval
(Murray & Nichols, 1948)

'Why can't young girls realise it's madly
dangerous to vamp most men!'

A Short History of Fingers, H Allen Smith
(Little Brown, 1963)

'Never stick your finger in a woman's business.'

Sorority Sluts, Jan Hudson
(Midwood, 1962)

'It was a lushly curved nymph of a teacher who taught him the real lessons.'

A Stress Analysis of the Strapless Evening Gown, Francis O Chisholm
(Prentice-Hall, 1963)

'When things are going well, something will go wrong and let you down.'

A Study of Masturbation, John Francis Meagher
(Bailliere, Tindall & Cox, 1924)

'Any recommendation to marry in order to cure this habit is abominably unfair.'

Suggestive Thoughts for Busy Workers, Osborne Keen
(Christian Book Room, 1883)

'Uplifting ideas for men and women to
practise daily.'

Syphilis: A Poetical History of the French Disease,
Nahum Tate (London, 1686)

'So delicately revealed it may be read by
the purest maidens.'

Tomcats in Tights, Jack Hanley
(Avon Books, 1955)

'They were two pussies who really knew how
to come on in Broadway.'

Tosser, Gunman, Frank Carr
(Ward Lock, 1939)

'Betty's fingers gripped her quirt tightly; she, too,
had heard of Tosser Smith.'

Twilight Girls: Down with Men!,
Judson Grey (Epic Originals, 1962)

'The lascivious, lady-lusting League of Amazons.'

Under Two Queens, John Skrine (Macmillan, 1884)

'His life was dedicated to the service of two
great beauties.'

Ups and Downs of Lady Di,
Annette Lyster (Brentano's, 1907)

'She little knew a handsome prince
would seal her fate.'

Warped Women, Jane Pritchard
(Lion Books, 1962)

'Strange love stripped them of all decency.'

What's Wrong with Bottoms?
P Hessell & J Nelson (Hutchinson, 1987)

'An amusing book for children with lots of coloured illustrations.'

Women on the Job, Judith Buber-Agassi
(Lexington Books, 1979)

'A lively account of the activities of professional women.'

Women's Worth, Anonymous
(London, seventeenth century)

'A treatise proving by sundry reasons that women do excel men.'

FIVE

WHAT'S THAT NOSHIN'
ON MY LEG?

Throw Away Titles that were Thrown Away

Over the years there have certainly been many books that have suffered from an improbable title, while just as many have benefited from a good one. In this context I am reminded of a story about one of my favourite horror novels, *Dr Jekyll and Mr Hyde*, told by the author himself, Robert Louis Stevenson, a man known to enjoy a play on words. While giving an interview in New York in 1887, Stevenson told a reporter who was mispronouncing the title that the name Jekyll should be pronounced with an initial long 'e' as in 'Geekill' but not as in 'Dzeckle' or 'Jeckel'. As Stevenson knew French, this suggests that the surname was intended to signify 'Je kill' meaning 'I kill' and hence the title of the novel had a special significance and could be read as 'I Kill and Hide'.

Ernest Hemingway was one author we know who devoted a lot of time to the titles of his stories and books – but did not give thought to them until after he had finished the work in progress. 'Sometimes I have as many as a hundred,' he was once quoted, 'then I start eliminating them – sometimes all of them.' Raymond Chandler was also always seeking the perfect title and kept a little notebook in which he jotted down any ideas that came to him. After his death, the book was found to contain dozens of wonderful titles that he never used, including *The Man with the Shredded Ear, Lament But No Tears* and *The Corpse Came in Person*.

In this chapter is a selection of some wonderful titles that might have adorned now very famous books, but were mercifully confined to oblivion before the presses rolled...

1813
First Impressions by Jane Austen

The rector's daughter, whose writing ranged from a satire on the Gothic fiction of her time to penetrating studies of human behaviour, had trouble finding the right title for one of the most enduring of all her books – until finally settling on the all-encompassing... *Pride and Prejudice.*

1818

Prometheus Unchained by Mary Shelley

The daughter of the feminist pioneer, Mary Wollstonecraft, Mary Shelley eloped with the poet Percy Shelley when she was still in her teens. While the pair were in Switzerland she wrote the novel about a scientist's creation of a man-made being, which could have appeared under this title until the inspired choice of her husband to call it... *Frankenstein.*

1844

Martin Sweetlewag by Charles Dickens

The great novelist was one of the most prolific creators of alternative titles for his stories, many of which were originally published as serials in magazines. This creativity was particularly furious after a visit to America in 1842 with the story that he called – apart from the above – Martin Sweetledew, then Martin Chuzzletow before deciding on... *Martin Chuzzlewit.*

1848

The Novel Without a Hero BY WILLIAM THACKERAY

Born in Calcutta, Thackeray dissipated his inheritance while still a young man, turned to journalism to make his way, and after a series of works under various pseudonyms – including Fitzbootle, Titmarsh and Snob – began the series of novels that made his name. His tale of a social climber making her way through the decadent upper classes of London was almost on the verge of being published when Thackeray had second thoughts – and suggested...*Vanity Fair.*

1853

Tom-All-Alone's Factory That Got into Chancery and Never Got Out BY CHARLES DICKENS

A mystery story of forgery, blackmail and murder that introduced Inspector Bucket, the first significant detective in English literature, provided Dickens with a similar headache when it came to a title and, apart from this long-winded version, he also considered *The Ruined House* and *The East Wind* before deciding on the simple...*Bleak House.*

1854

Two and Two Are Four BY CHARLES DICKENS

The evidence of a letter to his editor reveals that Dickens lavished even more possible titles on his next serial of unrelenting human misery, including *A Mere Question of Figures, Hard Heads and Soft Hearts, Prove It, Rust and Dust, Hard-Headed Gradgrind, According to Cocker* and – appropriately – *Stubborn Things*, until, finally, the solution was found in...*Hard Times.*

1857

Les Limbs BY CHARLES BAUDELAIRE

This was the French poet's original title for his group of macabre poems intended as an acknowledgment to the Limbo described in Dante Alighieri's *Divina Commedia*, until it changed following a suggestion by the critic Hippolyte Babou that it would sound better as...*Les Fleurs du Mal*.

1860

St. Ogg's on the Floss BY GEORGE ELIOT

Mary Ann Evans, who published her novels under the pseudonym 'George Eliot', discussed several alternative titles for her story of rural morality including this one, *Sister Maggie and The House of Tulliver* before finally accepting her publisher's suggestion – *The Mill on the Floss*.

1864

All's Well That Ends Well BY LEO TOLSTOY

The famous Russian novelist, philosopher and mystic led a dissolute life at university and on the family farm until he joined the army. Tolstoy's experiences in the Crimean War deeply affected him and a series of sketches and tales about the horrors of battle culminated in a book described as one of the greatest novels ever written. The author's initial title was *1805*, but when he abandoned any thoughts of a happy ending, he settled for the unsurpassable: *War and Peace*.

1880

Judah: A Tale of the Christ BY LEW WALLACE

Wallace, a soldier from Indiana who became the governor of Utah in 1878, spent years writing his novel about the violent birth of Christianity. Just before the book was published, it was suggested to him that a simpler title with more impact and sales appeal would be...*Ben-Hur.*

1883

The Sea-Cook BY ROBERT LOUIS STEVENSON

The Scottish-born author, who briefly trained to follow his family profession as an engineer, instead travelled and made his name with essays and tales based on his experiences in Europe and America. His fame was assured by the high adventure tale about a search for a pirate's buried loot that he was advised to retitle...*Treasure Island.*

1891

The Body and Soul of Sue BY THOMAS HARDY

An architect turned writer, Hardy brilliantly portrayed both the underside of rural life and its idylls in his series of Wessex novels. The powerful story of one of his doomed heroines went through several other titles including *Too Late, Beloved* and *Tess of the Hardys* before appearing as...*Tess of the D'Urbervilles.*

1895

Private Fleming, His Various Battles BY STEPHEN CRANE

The American writer and war correspondent, who switched from writing stories of urban life to tales set on the battlefield, made a last-minute decision to alter the title of his Civil War epic and came up with – *The Red Badge of Courage.*

1896

The Recalcitrants BY THOMAS HARDY

Hardy again considered several titles when he completed his explicit novel about a man made an outcast because of his shocking behaviour. Initially called *The Simpleton,* it went through *The Recalcitrants* to *Hearts Insurgent,* before finally reaching the presses as... *Jude the Obscure.*

1897

The Un-Dead BY BRAM STOKER

Irish-born Abraham Stoker worked as a clerk and then for many years as manager to the actor Sir Henry Irving, only having time for his writing when off duty. Without even visiting the setting of his story about a vampire count in Transylvania, he created arguably the most famous horror novel of all – making a rapid title change just before the manuscript was to be printed to the immortal...*Dracula.*

1903

Ernest Pontifex BY SAMUEL BUTLER

The English author, painter and musician famous during his lifetime for his Utopian satire, *Erewhon* (1872) – the title is (almost) an inversion of 'nowhere' – did not live to see the publication of his final novel about four generations of an ill-starred family earn him a place in literary history after a title change to...*The Way of All Flesh*.

1905

From a Sense of Duty BY E M FORSTER

The academic Forster became famous for his stories of English middle-class life during the first decade of the century with their special insight into public schools, the church and the civil service. His first novel, set in Italy, was submitted as a serial under the title, *Monteriano*, renamed *From a Sense of Duty*, but it was ultimately published as... *Where Angels Fear to Tread*.

1915

The Saddest Story BY FORD MADOX FORD

This English-born writer was gassed in the early months of the First World War, but survived to write several atmospheric novels about the conflict plus some fine poetry. Although his classic love story did not feature the war at all, the title was deliberately changed to sound more patriotic in war-torn Britain: *The Good Soldier*.

1920

The Village Virus BY SINCLAIR LEWIS

The son of a doctor, Lewis became a journalist and made his reputation with books exposing the intolerance and materialism of American society that began with this story of hypocrisy in a small community. On publication, the retitled book was widely condemned, but still gave a new expression to the language...*Main Street.*

1925

Trimalchio in West Egg BY F SCOTT FITZGERALD

Fitzgerald, who would become labelled as the chronicler of the 'Jazz Age', had problems with the titles of several of his books, notably his tale of sex and debauchery among the super-rich on Long Island. After objections by his publishers to this title, other suggestions included *The High-bouncing Lover* and *Gold-Batted Gatsby* before the final choice was made: *The Great Gatsby.*

1925

Four Years of Struggle Against Lies, Stupidity and Cowardice BY ADOLF HITLER

The extraordinary testimony of a man hell-bent on world-domination was dictated to one of his acolytes, Rudolph Hess, while the author was serving nine months' imprisonment in Landsberg Jail in Germany. The pernicious volume might even have disappeared without trace, but for the inexorable rise of its author and a title change to...*Mein Kampf (My Struggle).*

1928

John Thomas and Lady Jane BY D H LAWRENCE

The son of a miner, this great English novelist, who achieved success with his first novel, *The White Peacock* (1911), laboured over the titles of most of his books. His classic tale of illicit love between the classes, later prosecuted for obscenity, had its title changed from the original to...*Lady Chatterley's Lover.*

1933

Wives of Geniuses I Have Sat With BY GERTRUDE STEIN

This American author, whose salon and patronage of the arts in Paris in the early years of the twentieth century was hugely influential on many writers, always had trouble with her titles, especially with her autobiographical works. The title destined to ensure Stein's reputation – featuring her lifelong companion whose notorious cookbook contained a recipe for 'Hashish Brownies' – veered from *My Life with the Great* to *My 25 Years with Gertrude Stein* to the enduring...*The Autobiography of Alice B. Toklas.*

1934

Bar B-Q BY JAMES M CAIN

A newspaperman and political columnist until the 1930s, Cain then wrote what would make him a legend in crime fiction. The novel about a young drifter and his attraction for the sexy wife of a rural café owner, which results in the pair plotting to murder the old man, was finally published as...*The Postman Always Rings Twice.*

1935

The Lost BY CHRISTOPHER ISHERWOOD

The English novelist who became famous for stories based on his time as a tutor in the decadence of post-slump, pre-Hitler Berlin, saw his work go through title changes after his original choice. *The Lost* gave way to the more evocative, *The Last of Mr Norris*, the omnibus volume, *Berlin Tales*, and finally...*I Am a Camera*.

1936

Ba! Ba! Black Sheep BY MARGARET MITCHELL

Mitchell, who was born in Atlanta, Georgia, studied medicine for a while before turning to journalism, and then spent years creating one of the most popular and influential novels of the century. The story, with its Civil War background, began life as *Pansy*, was then rapidly changed from *Milestones* to *Tote the Weary Load, Tomorrow Is Another Day* – even *Ba! Ba! Black Sheep* – before the immortal *Gone with the Wind* was chosen.

1937

Something That Happened BY JOHN STEINBECK

An American writer revered for his realistic, compassionate novels of lowly people, Steinbeck created two unforgettable characters in this tale of the mentally retarded big man, Lennie, and his little friend, George. Unhappy with the working title, Steinbeck found the phrase that really summarised the plot in a Robert Burns poem: *Of Mice and Men*.

1940

The Mute BY CARSON MCCULLERS

The American novelist McCullers, who was born in Georgia and wrote psychological tales set mainly in her native South, was encouraged to change the original title of what proved to be her masterpiece to – *The Heart is a Lonely Hunter.*

1940

Zounds, He Dies BY RAYMOND CHANDLER

The English-born master of American hard-boiled fiction changed the titles of several of his books, perhaps none more dramatically than this Philip Marlowe case inspired by Shakespeare's *Richard III*. He apparently also debated over *The Second Murderer* and *Sweet Bells Jangle*, before the choice was finally made for...*Farewell, My Lovely.*

1941

Three Tenant Families BY JAMES AGEE

The memorable collaboration of this American writer with photographer Walker Evans highlighted the plight of poor workers in words and pictures; it was published under the evocative Biblical quote: *Let Us Now Praise Famous Men.*

1942

The Brasher Doubloon BY RAYMOND CHANDLER

Chandler and his editor had several exchanges about the proposed title for another of his greatest thrillers – during which *The Brasher Doubloon* was proposed and rejected because of a fear that 'Brasher' (an ancient coin) might get pronounced as 'Brassiere'. The final vote went to...*The High Window.*

1945

The House of the Faith BY EVELYN WAUGH

The irascible English author of some of the most sardonic and entertaining books about the social life of the country from the 1920s onwards might not, perhaps, have had one of his greatest successes without a title change to: *Brideshead Revisited.*

1947

Blanche's Chair in the Moon BY TENNESSEE WILLIAMS

This American dramatist, who also wrote some fine short stories and novels, puzzled over the titles of many of his works, including his powerful erotic drama about a faded New Orleans belle. Originally entitled *The Moth*, the play was also referred to by the girl's name as well as *The Poker Night*, before its final version that won a Pulitzer Prize: *A Streetcar Named Desire.*

1949

The Last Man in Europe BY GEORGE ORWELL

Born in Bengal, Orwell served for some years in the Indian police before fighting in the Spanish Civil War and acting as a war correspondent during the Second World War – all of which inspired his later work. This title for his classic novel about a scientifically perfected servile state remained until just before publication when Orwell decided to postpone his awful prophecy by simply reversing the date he had written it: *Nineteen Eighty-Four*.

1951

If Wishes Were Horses BY JAMES JONES

The American author of two of the greatest novels of the Second World War agonised over the title for his first book about life in a heaving, unsettled army camp. This version was rejected, along with *Old Soldiers Never Die* and *They Merely Fade Away*, before Jones and his publisher agreed on – *From Here to Eternity*.

1954

Llareggub BY DYLAN THOMAS

The Welsh-born poet and short-story writer whose lifestyle scandalised many people – though it also helped to ensure his legend – rose to international fame with a wonderful evocation of small-town Welsh life that he initially called *Quite Early One Morning*. However, his irreverent sense of humour made him change the title to that of his fictional community – read it backwards – until he was persuaded to use the more acceptable: *Under Milk Wood*.

1955

The Kingdom by the Sea BY VLADIMIR NABOKOV

The hugely controversial novel by the Russian author about a middle-aged man's infatuation with a precociously experienced young girl, began its life with the heroine named Virginia and the book to be called Ginny. For a time she was renamed Juanita Dark, before making the final transformation into the teenage femme fatale – and becoming the unforgettable – *Lolita*.

1956

Finnerty's Ball BY NELSON ALGREN

The second of Algren's harsh portraits of the underworld of Chicago went through a second title change to *Somebody in Boots* until the author and publisher agreed upon – *A Walk on the Wild Side.*

1961

Catch-14 BY JOSEPH HELLER

Heller's classic American anti-war satire, which ultimately provided a famous catch phrase, actually went through two title changes before reaching the bookstalls. The author's original title was *Catch-14*. This was changed to *Catch-18* as publication neared, but then hastily retitled to avoid confusion with another forthcoming title, *Mila 18* by Leon Uris. The book finally made it with...*Catch-22*.

1962

Sex for the Single Woman BY HELEN GURLEY BROWN

This ground-breaking book by the editor of the American magazine, *Cosmopolitan*, had its title changed before going to press when Brown was told her title was rather too 'immoral'. Instead it became...*Sex and the Single Woman*.

1963

The Yo-Yo World of Benny Profane BY THOMAS PYNCHON

The enigmatic American writer, whose identity has for years been the subject of much debate, broke into print with a bestseller about a man every bit as mysterious as his creator. The manuscript was entitled *Low Lands*, but was subsequently given several new versions including *World on a String*, *The Quest of Herbert Strencil*, *Blood's a Rover*, *Of a Fond Ghoul*, *The Republican Party Is a Machine* and *Dream Tonight of Peacock Tails*, before the ultimate in simplicity was chosen: *V*.

1964

The Parts Nobody Knows BY ERNEST HEMINGWAY

Hemingway confessed to listing dozens of possible titles for his books, but did not live to see the final version of his last work. This account of his life as a tyro writer in Paris in the twenties could alternatively have been known as *It Is Different in the Ring*, *The Eye and the Ear*, *Love Is Hunger* and *To Write It Truly* – but it was Hemingway's widow, Mary, who settled the issue with...*A Moveable Feast*.

1968

They Don't Build Statues to Businessmen
BY JACQUELINE SUSANN

An American journalist's sensational novel of the sex and drugs lifestyle of a group of women in the swinging sixties is another book of the period that would probably never have achieved its millions of sales without a title change to – *Valley of the Dolls.*

1969

The Birds and the Bees BY DAVID R REUBEN

This revolutionary book about the latest medical and scientific discoveries to enable sexual pleasure to be more exciting, fulfilling and safer would have been published with a rather innocuous title except for a last-minute change to what is now a catch phrase: *Everything You Always Wanted to Know About Sex – But Were Afraid to Ask.*

1972

Come and Go BY XAVIERA HOLLANDER

Described as one of the books that helped to bring sex out of the closet, it told the story of the most influential madam in New York and proved a landmark in the struggle for sexual freedom. The eventual sales in excess of 16 million were undoubtedly helped by the title change to... *The Happy Hooker.*

1974

What's That Noshin' on My Leg? BY PETER BENCHLEY

Benchley's famous novel of one man's obsessive hunt for a marine killer was given several dozen titles – including *A Silence in the Water*, *Leviathan Rising*, *Great White*, *The Shark*, even this not-altogether serious suggestion from the author's father, Nathaniel Benchley – before an unbeatable solution surfaced: *Jaws*.

1974

At This Point in Time BY BOB WOODWARD & CARL BERNSTEIN

The book that brought down President Nixon described in relentless detail how the machinations of what became known as 'The Watergate Scandal' were painstakingly unearthed by two reporters on the *Washington Post*, but probably owed its ultimate success to the title change to...*All The President's Men*.

1977

Before This Anger BY ALEX HALEY

Another landmark book, by a black author who traced his origins back to Africa and focused attention on the plight of his people in America. The work went through several title changes before finally being published as...*Roots*.

1985

Panasonic BY DON DELILLO

An unsettling novel about America's consumer culture and the use of powerful advertising slogans, this book included references to many of them during the course of the narrative and DeLillo originally picked the name of the Japanese electronic giant for his title. When the company's lawyers threatened a suit for trademark infringement, a safer alternative was chosen: *White Noise*.

2003

If You Don't Have Big Breasts, Put Ribbons on Your Pigtails BY BARBARA CORCORAN

Corcoran, a Manhattan real estate broker, drew on childhood lessons from her mother and her experiences in New York to write this celebrated self-help book about getting on in business. Ultimately, however, she acceded to the wishes of her publishers that the title might prove too provocative and changed it to...*Use What You've Got & Other Business Lessons I Learned*.

2005

Forks BY STEPHENIE MEYER

Stephenie Meyer's dream of a story of teenage love and lust between vampire Edward and Bella came true in 2005 when her manuscript for *Forks* – named after the rainiest town in the USA – was picked up by a literary agent. Despite having a soft spot for this particular title it was decided unsuitable for a tale of forbidden desire. Instead, it was replaced by...*Twilight*.

SIX

THE PENIS MIGHTIER
THAN THE SWORD

Literary Graffiti from the World's Walls

No book such as this could possibly exist without a chapter devoted to graffiti, the compelling art of defacement created by a secretive army of anonymous writers. It should be no surprise that great books and authors have been the subject of many of these uniquely stylish and meaningful messages, which may be referred to in a parody of Jack London as 'The Scrawls of the Wild'. One of the earliest that sticks in my mind was to be found in the Reading Room of the British Museum, where a cheeky wag had written, 'It's a funny old world – Karl Marx.'

In fact, nameless scribes have been writing these compelling messages since the time of the Roman Empire – the word graffiti derives from the Italian 'graffio' meaning 'a scratch' – and a classic example came to light in the late eighteenth century when the ruins of Pompeii were being excavated. Underneath the detritus caused by the fatal eruption of Vesuvius was found a Latin inscription that stated with wonderful erotic enthusiasm, 'May I always have it off as well as I had it off here!' Subsequent generations have produced their own heroes, notably the ubiquitous Kilroy, who has apparently been here, there and everywhere since the middle of the twentieth century. The origin of the famous line, 'Kilroy was Here,' is undoubtedly American and can be reliably traced to the hand of a shipyard inspector, James J Kilroy, whose job was to inspect ships being built in Quincy, Massachusetts, during the Second World War. Before long, the phrase had spread far beyond the bounds of the shipyard and was often accompanied by a simple sketch of a face with a large nose peering over a wall (a figure that became known in the UK as 'Chad').

Today, the folklore surrounding graffiti is multiplying by the year, and some lines of graffiti have even inspired the titles of bestselling books and theatrical productions, including Edward Albee's *Who's Afraid of Virginia Woolf?* – found in a subway – while Anthony Newley spotted the title of his play, *Stop The World, I Want To Get Off* on a London wall. The examples that I have collected here are probably not going to generate quite such fame but their literary humour is certainly priceless!

Agatha Christie has died – whodunnit?

A dictionary is the only place
where success comes before work

All men eat but Fu Manchu

Anagrams lure, OK

Anyone for Tennyson?

Auden was very Audenry

Back in a minute – Godot

Bad spellers of the world, untie!

Biggles Flies Undone

Confucius he say too much

Cunnilingus spoken here

The days of good English has went

*Dr Strangelove; or, How I
Learned to Love the Bum*

Dracula – your Bloody Mary is ready

Fiction is a fact

*Flash Gordon exposes himself to all
sorts of perils for mankind*

Genitals Prefer Blondes

George Orwell was an optimist

Graffiti is squatters' writes

God is dead – Nietzsche

Nietzsche is dead – God

Home Rule for Wales – and Moby Dick for King!

Humpty Dumpty was pushed

*— I am, therefore I think — Is this putting Descartes
before the horse?*

I choked Linda Lovelace

*I thought Fellatio was a character in Hamlet until I
discovered Smirnoff*

*If pornography relieves sexual frustration —
give cookbooks to the hungry*

Illiterates watch this space

—•—

Immanuel Kant but Kubla Khan

—•—

—

Is Hamlet the son of Piglet?

—•—

'It's a lie – I was never here,' Kilroy

—•—

I've been hanging around here for ages – Godot

—•—

James Bond Rules OOK?

MI5 – the origin of spieses

Mr Kipling writes exceedingly good books

Lassie Kills Chickens

Little Red Riding Hood is a Russian contraceptive

*Mary Poppins shouldn't fly
around without knickers*

1978 makes 1984 look like 1967

*Norman Mailer is the master of the
single entendre*

*Oedipus was the first man to plug
the generation gap*

Ogden Nash is trash

Oust Proust!

The penis mightier than the sword

Poetry is when every
Line starts with a
Capital letter

Printers do it and don't wrinkle the sheets

Quasimodo – that name rings a bell

Roget's Thesaurus rules – dominates,
regulates, all right, OK

Samuel Beckett is Krapp

Shakespeare used bard language – but Anne hath a way with him!

Sherlock Holmes for deduction – Casanova for reproduction

Typographers rule, OQ

Watership Down – You've read the book, seen the film, now eat the pie!

SEVEN

RAMBO WAS A
FAMOUS FRENCH POET

Classroom Howlers and Schoolboy Exam Errors

For several years while I was working in publishing I lived near Highgate and it was there I first heard about a legendary collector and writer on howlers, Cecil Hunt. He had earned the soubriquet 'The Howler King of Highgate' as a result of a series of books he had compiled beginning in 1927 with *Howlers* and swelling to half a dozen volumes by the time he reached *Hand-Picked Howlers* in 1937 and *Ripe Howlers* two years later.

Cecil Hunt's early sources were mainly junior schools, but he went on to include grammar schools and even, on occasions, universities. I had hours of fun dipping into these books, and one particular item set me off collecting those with a literary inspiration. It was written by a London schoolboy, apparently: 'Writers are very strange because teacher says tails come out of their heads.' To Cecil Hunt, these errors from the classroom and the examination hall represented a 'form of humour that is without malice and is alive with humanity'.

What 'The Howler King of Highgate' initiated, I have continued in more recent years, collecting literary howlers from all over the world and adding material from such diverse sources as evening classes and correspondence courses – revealing that adults can slip up just as comically as youngsters. Even examiners can occasionally get it wrong, as one paper sent to me demonstrated: 'Examinations may be written or vice versa.' My selection begins with Shakespeare, primarily because the poor fellow has probably suffered more from literary howlers than anyone else...

The greatest writer of the Renaissance was William Shakespeare. He was born in the year 1564, supposedly on his birthday. He wrote tragedies, comedies and hysterectomies, all in Islamic pentameter.

Five of Shakespeare's best plays are *Macbeth*, *The Mikado*, *Quo Vadis*, *San Toy* and *The Sign of the Cross*.

Shakespeare married Anne Hathaway who, it seems, lived up to her name and had her own way and gave Shakespeare a hot time of it.

Shakespeare lived in Windsor with his merry wives.

In Shakespeare's *A Midsummer Night's Dream*, Puck turns Bottom's head into an ass.

In the play, Bottom, as his name suggests, behaves in a very bumptious manner.

Romeo met Juliet for the first time at
the massacred ball.

Romeo had to keep walking under Juliet's bed.
This is one of his greatest tragedies.

Romeo's last wish was to be laid by Juliet.

The Merchant of Venice was a famous Italian who
bought and sold canal boats.

'To be or not to be; that is the question.' Nobody
knows what this means because many words
Shakespeare wrote now mean something else.

Cyclops wrote the *Encyclopaedia*.

Q: In what circumstances does the Fourth
Act of *Hamlet* begin?

A: It commences immediately after the Third Act.

—•—

Macbeth was Dick Turpin's horse.

—•—

Prospero had a faithful friend called Gorgonzola.

—•—

Hamlet stabbed Ophelia's father Polyphemus
who was hiding behind the fireplace.

—•—

Macduff said he had never been born of a woman
because he had been stolen when he was a baby.

—•—

Bacon was the man who thought
he wrote Shakespeare.

—•—

Plato's Republic was another name for the infernal regions.

———

Homer wrote The Oddity.

———

Virgil was in love with a girl named Enid and wrote lots of books about her.

———

Livid was a famous Roman poet.

———

Socrates died from an overdose of wedlock.

———

Algebra is the wife of Euclid.

———

The Compleat Angler is another name for Euclid, who wrote all about angles.

———

In the first book of the *Bible*, Guinessis,
Adam and Eve were created from an apple tree.

———

Moses went up on Mount Cyanide to get the Ten
Commandments.

———

According to the *Bible*, Jesus was born because Mary
had an immaculate contraption.

———

Gutenberg invented removable type and the *Bible*.

———

John Wycliff's great work was the translation of the
Bible into Middle English because he thought the
people would be more likely to understand the English
as spoken in the Midlands.

———

William the Conqueror is one of our foremost authors
and wrote the *Domesday Book*.

———

The Domesday Book is a book which tells about the animals in the country. It has got in it how many tadpoles there are in a pond.

Cicero was banished to Macedonia where he wrote the Book of Lamentations.

A fairy tale is something that never happened a long time ago.

A sentence is a short conversation.

The definition of 'prose' is men who get paid for playing cricket.

In every book there is a hero and a heroine and they are called the heroic couplet.

The hero of the story was clad in a shining suet of arm.

Autobiography is the history of motor cars.

The objective of 'He' is 'She'.

Q: Give three adverbs ending in '-where'.

A: Somewhere, Nowhere and Earthenwhere.

'Ster' is a feminine suffix, as will be seen
in spinster, monster and sterile.

A passive verb is when the subject is
the sufferer, as 'I am loved'.

A metaphor is a kind of signalling used
chiefly for long distances.

Poetic License was a License granted to poets allowing
them to recite their poems in public houses.

Rambo was a famous French poet.

A catalogue is a dialogue by four people.

The death of Julius Caesar was foretold by
a shower of metaphors.

In the reign of King George the Second according to
the history books the good old days were taking place.

James the First wrote a few books which
were unfit to read.

In 1663, Milton married and afterwards he wrote
Paradise Lost. Later his wife died and he then wrote
Paradise Regained.

Chaucer was the father of English pottery.

Chaucer wrote the *Arabian Knights* who were holy men like Prince Arthur and made pilgrimages to Canterbury and told tales round a table.

When Chaucer described the Prioress as amiable of port he meant she was fond of wine.

Coleridge was a retired mariner who took to verse and wrote Ku-Klux-Klan.

Kubla Khan is an American secret society.

Charles Darwin was the originator of the human species and wrote a lot about it.

Darwin was the author of a famous book called *Tarzan of the Apes*.

Ganymede and Runnymede were two characters by Charles Dickens.

The only Englishman who became Pope of Rome was Nicholas Nickleby.

———•———

In the olden days, little boys didn't have any fathers and mothers, so Oliver Twist had to be born in a workhouse.

———•———

The ghost of Bob Marley visited Ebenezer Scrooge.

———•———

Edgar Allan Poe was a curdling writer.

———•———

Edgar Allan Poe was born in Boston in 1809 and was found unconscious. Three days later, he died in 1849.

———•———

Twenty-thousand Leagues Under the Sea is a book about a lot of underwater football teams.

———•———

In *Little Women* Amy had an air of refinery about her.

———•———

Robinson Crusoe was a sailor who got stuck on an uninhibited island without even a television.

———

As he grew older, Wordsworth went out one evening because he felt the call of nature.

———

F Scott Fitzgerald's *The Great Gatsby* exemplified American culture in the 1920s to a tea.

———

H G Wells' *Outline of History* is a veritable millstone on the road to learning.

———

In 1957, Eugene O'Neill won a Pullet Surprise.

———

At the start of *The Grapes of Wrath,* Oklahoma has been hit by a dust bowl.

———

Jake Barnes in *The Sun Also Rises,* was injured in the groin region and was impudent for the rest of his life.

The theme of The *Catcher in the Rye* is that Holden Caulfield leaves the world of childhood and enters the world of adultery.

A Plagiarist is a writer of plays.

Letters in sloping type are in hysterics.

An antidote is a funny story you have heard before.

Euphemism is a thing which is not done by people, e.g. mew, woof or cock-a-doodle.

A collective noun is a noun that covers everything, such as clothing, umbrella, bandstand, etc.

A mixed metaphor means putting the wrong halves of proverbs together, such as 'Too many cooks make an ill wind' or 'A spoilt broth blows nobody any good'.

Terminology is a science which deals
with the ends of words.

—•—

The author's story is very aboriginal.

—•—

When it used to say in books that a man carried
his mistress's favour on his arm, it meant that he
carried the baby on his arm.

—•—

In crime stories, the detective is a man who searches
out the mysteries of things in his private clothes.

—•—

A comma is what a medium falls into.

—•—

A colon is a punctuation mark in the human body.

—•—

Ambiguity means writing the truth
when you don't want to.

—•—

Poets no longer wear long hair and dirty clothes, but they still expect people to read what they have written.

The Bodleian is a type of harp.

The Highway Code is a book of rules for walkers who are run over.

An appendix is the portion of a book that nobody has yet discovered to be of any use.

EIGHT

THOU SHALT COMMIT ADULTERY

The Bible and the Printer's Devil

I read somewhere that there is only one joke in the Bible. I am not sure *what* story is being referred to, but in actual fact the book contains quite a number of amusing episodes – ranging from those about the Old Testament prophets who indulged in eating scrolls (Ezekiel, iii) and hiding underwear beneath rocks (Jeremiah, xiii) to the comic misadventures of Balaam's ass (Numbers, xxii). Jesus also had a ready store of one-liners for suitable moments, including such gems as 'The poor always ye have with you' and 'the blind leading the blind'. I'm also unable to resist smiling at another particular line from Job xxxi, 35: 'Oh that mine adversary had written a book.'

The Bible itself has also inspired some amusing stories among the literary fraternity, like that concerning Thomas Mitchell, who was discovered on his deathbed reading a copy and when asked what he was doing, replied: 'Looking for a loophole.' There was also the dying classical scholar, Arthur Bernard Cook, who while he was being read to from the 121st Psalm protested, 'That is a mistranslation!' And there is something irredeemably comic about the eccentric Victorian vicar of Bremhill, William Bowles, who presented one of his friends with a copy of the Bible inscribed, 'With the Author's Compliments'. And I must not forget to mention the enterprising publisher who not so long ago advertised his edition of the Bible with a jingle that ran:

> *Holy Scripture, Writ Divine,*
> *Leather-bound at one and nine.*
> *Satan trembles when he sees,*
> *Bibles sold as cheap as these.*

Over the centuries, the Bible has been published in countless editions and translations, not overlooking those in shorthand – issued by Jeremy Rich, c. 1665 – and even hieroglyphics in 1785, when small pictures were used instead of specific words and phrases. The Bible has also suffered more than most books at the hands of its printers and there is, for example, a copy of an eighteenth-century edition on display in Westminster Abbey which is aptly known as the 'Printer's Bible'. A line in Psalms, cxix, 161, reads, 'Printers have persecuted me without a cause.' The word should, of course, be 'Princes'. This is, though, by no means the worst misprint, and here are some of the most amusing examples of the intervention of the Printer's Devil that have resulted in some *very* Unauthorised Versions of the good book...

And Adam and Eve sewed fig leaves together and made themselves breeches [*clothes*].

Genesis, iii, 7 – Geneva, 1534

Thou shalt not need to be afraid for any bugges [*terror*] by night.

Psalms, xci, 5 – Coverdale, 1535

Blessed are the placemakers [*peacemakers*].

Matthew, v, 9 – London, 1562

Christ condemneth [*commendeth*]
the poore widdowe.

Luke, xxi, 1 – London, 1562

Is there no treacle [*balm*] in Gilead.

Jeremiah, viii, 22 – Coverdale, 1568

Then said Judas [*Jesus*] unto the twelve.

John, vi, 67 – London, 1611

Thou shalt [*not*] commit adultery.

Exodus, xx, 14 – Blackfriars, 1632

The fool hath said in his heart,
there is [*no*] God.

Psalms, xiv, 1 – London, 1634

Her sins, which are many, are forgotten [*forgiven*].

Luke, vii, 47 – Cambridge, 1638

Know ye that the unrighteous shall [*not*] inherit the kingdom of God?

I Corinthians, vi, 9 – London, 1653

Neither yield ye your members as instruments of [*un*]righteousness unto sin.

Romans, vi, 13 – London, 1653

I have seen thine adversaries [*adulteries*].

Jeremiah, xiii, 27 – London, 1682

Therefore deliver up their children to the swine [*famine*].

Jeremiah, vxiii, 21 – London, 1682

And if the latter husband [*h*]ate her.

Deuteronomy, xxiv, 3 – London, 1682

For without are dogs, and scorers [*sorcerers*].

Revelation, xxii, 15 – Clarendon, 1702

Behold, thou art made whole:
sin on [*no*] more.

John, v, 14 – Oxford, 1716

The Parable of the Vinegar [*Vineyard*].

Luke, xx – London, 1724

The sting [*string*] of his tongue.

Mark, vii, 35 – Edinburgh, 1747

Ye Blind guides which strain out
[*at*] a gnat.

Matthew, xxii, 24 – Cambridge, 1760

———

Their land brought forth frogs, yea seven [*even*] in
their king's chamber.

Psalms, v, 30 – London, 1778

———

Let the children first be killed [*filled*].

Mark, vii, 27 – Winchester, 1795

———

These are murderers [*murmurers*].

Jude, xvi, 16 – Canterbury, 1801

———

For the flesh lusteth after [*against*] the Spirit.

Galatians, v, 17 – London, 1804

———

But thy son that shall come forth out
of thy lions [*loins*].

I Kings, viii, 19 – London, 1804

———•———

The murderers shall surely be put together
[*to death*].

Numbers, xxxv, 18 – London, 1804

———•———

I discharge [*charge*] thee before God.

Timothy, v, 21 – London, 1806

———•———

Who hath ears to [*h*]ear, let him hear.

Matthew, xiii, 43 – Cambridge, 1807

———•———

If any man come to me, and hate not his father and
mother, yea and his own wife [*life*] also.

Luke, xiv, 26 – London, 1812

And it shall come to pass, that the fishes
[*fishers*] shall stand.

Ezekiel, xiv, 19 – London, 1816

———

Shall I bring to the birth, and not cease [*cause*]
to bring forth.

Isiah, xvi, 9 – Oxford, 1820

———

And Rebekah arose, and her camels [*damsels*].

Genesis, xxiv, 61 – London, 1823

———

For Christ also hath once offered
[*suffered*] for our sins.

Peter, iii, 18 – London, 1824

———

Rejoice and be exceeding clad [*glad*].

Matthew, v, 12 – York, 1864

A man may not marry his
grandmother's wife.

Table of Affinity, Oxford University Press, 1923

———

Pay [*Pray*] for peace.

Psalm 122, 6 – Jerusalem Bible, 1966

———

NINE

ENGLISH AS SHE IS WROTTEN

Very Lost in Translation

The guidebook industry has become big business in the last couple of centuries as methods of transport have improved and the desire of people to travel further afield has increased every year. Alongside the growth of this interest have come an ever-increasing number of guidebooks to inform and instruct tourists about the places to visit. One of the greatest pitfalls for such guides lies in translation, which has resulted in some glaring errors, not to mention very amusing mistakes. This fact was familiar to Charles Berlitz, the man who founded the famous institution bearing his name, Berlitz Language Schools, and has recently been commented on again by his grandson, also Charles Berlitz, in his book, *Native Tongues*, in which he offers many little-known facts and anecdotes about languages. Among the most fascinating is that German could have been the official language of the United States if the proposal had not been defeated by just one vote at the Continental Conference in Philadelphia in 1787. He also lists a number of curious examples of the foibles of translation, citing the well-known English proverb 'Don't count your chickens before they are hatched' becoming in German 'You can't hang people before you've caught them', and the delicate matter of complimenting a Japanese woman on her beauty where her face must be compared to 'an egg with eyes'.

Such variations in the nuances of words and phrases have led to some comic mistranslations, as you will discover in this chapter.

The Elements of French Translation

John Perrin (1820)

This book, published in Paris early in the nineteenth century, is one of the earliest I have been able to trace and was evidently popular, as the publisher claims it ran to 21 editions. The following phrases were apparently repeated through many of the printings and Mr Perrin's work might fairly be said to have set the standard for all the writers and publishers who followed in his footsteps.

Ayez soin de la retaper proprement – Take care to cock it up neatly.
Cortège – A small house in the country.
Deshabiller – To give up a bad habit.
Du jambon cru – What was supposed to be ham.
Elle a mal au coeur – She is rotten to the core.
Elles sont venues – The girls have come.
Emporté par la colère – Carried off by the collar.
Feu la reine – Shoot the Queen.
Hors d'oeuvre – Out of work.
Huile d'olivier – Oily oblivion.
Il a un crêpe au chapeau – He has crept into his hat.
J'ai hâte de l'embrasser – I hate to embrace her.
La lueur argentée de la lune – The moneyed light of the moon.
La jeune fille avait acquis plus de poids dans les conseils de la famille – According to the girl's family, she was bought more by weight.
Laisser-faire – An idle French woman.
Le livre est un bon un – The book is a good one.
Menage à trois – To share the burden.
Mes souvenirs sont peu précis – My recollections are precious few.
Prenez garde que votre cheval ne prenne pas le mors entre les dents – Take care that your horse does not die of the toothache.
Savoir faire – To know a good thing.
Spectacles théâtrales – Opera glasses.
Un homme mange plus d'une femme – A man eats more than a woman.

Conversation for Occupying Forces

German Army Information Bureau (1940)

During the Second World War when the German Army had reached the French coast and an invasion of Britain seemed imminent in the summer of 1940, a phrase book in German and English was prepared in Berlin for the Nazi troops. Copies of this subsequently came into the possession of British Intelligence from the occupied Channel Islands and revealed typical Teutonic thoroughness in preparing their force for dealing with the English population and their idiosyncrasies. They were to demand that the local population tell them the truth as they overran the nation – and to shoot anyone who told a lie.

Here are some typical suggestions:

– *Are you the mayor?*
– *Open all the cupboards!*
– *Where is the cash?*
– *Write down the amount in the safe.*
– *I shall confiscate all this money!*
– *Show me the way to your house.*
– *I will board and lodge here.*
– *You will wash two shirts, one pair of trousers and three pocket-handkerchiefs.*
– *We shall need your horses and carts.*
– *If you drive the wrong way you will be shot.*
– *I have the stomach ache.*
– *I need pills.*
– *Give me opium.*

Know Your Comrades in Arms!

Pravda Phrasebook (1948)

In the aftermath of the Second World War when the English and American forces jointly occupied Germany with Soviet troops, a Russian–English language guide was prepared by the nation's leading newspaper for distribution to the men. Although the booklet provided many useful terms, underlying some of the phrases was the Russian state's paranoia about the intents of their allies, as this selection of some typical entries shows.

– *Please give me fried chicks, pulled bread and sower cream.*

– *I would like some curds and one jelly-fish.*

– *How is accommodation for you?*

– *Do you have a bed and room to wash and shit?*

– *I want my hair frizzled.*

– *Do you jerk in your jeep?*

– *Flying in the TU-114 I felt myself excellently.*

– *The woman here are poisonous?*

– *Whose invention is this?*

– *This is a Soviet invention!*

– *How powerful is this reactor?*

– *Show me a working diagram of this reactor.*

– *Do you have a device for outer space research work?*

Instructions for Motorists

Tokyo Information Bureau (1960)

The advent of major tourism from Western Europe and America to Japanese cities inspired several guide and phrase books, which were prepared with painstaking care but an understandable paucity of knowledge of the English language and customs. Nowhere was this perhaps more evident than in the section of the Tokyo booklet about motoring customs in Japanese cities.

At the rise of the hand of policeman, stop rapidly.
Do not pass him or otherwise disrespect him.

When a passenger of the foot hove in sight, tootle to him melodiously at first. If the passenger still obstacles your passage, tootle him with vigour and express by word of mouth the warning, 'Hi! Hi!'

Beware the wandering horse, that he shall not take fright as you pass him. Do not explode the exhaust box at him. Go soothingly by, or stop by the roadside till he pass away.

Give big space to the festive dog that makes sport in the roadway. Avoid entanglement of dog with your wheel spokes.

Go soothingly on the grease-mud, as there lurk the skid demon.

Press the brake of foot as you roll round the corners to save the collapse and tie-up.

Teach Yourself English

Jesus Rodrigues (Rio de Janeiro, 1971)

Brazil – and South America in general – has also seen a huge increase in the number of tourists in recent years and again willing authors and publishers have stepped forward with guidebooks of varying degrees of proficiency. This book, which contained an amazing list of what it described as 'everyday vocabulary' – from 'Easter' to 'strike-breaking' and including 'ostrich', 'pimp' and the even more curious 'forget it' and 'lack of show off' – devoted a section to the country's beautiful girls and their menfolk with an expressive list of phrases in Portuguese and English:

– *Who is that girl near your brother?*

– *She is a glamour-girl. She has been in the jungle for ten years.*

– *Are the other two fellows connections of hers?*

– *No, one is a big-shot and the other is a cake-eater.*

– *That flapper seems to be a gold-digger – am I right?*

– *That is right. She left the poor boy embroiled.*

– *Is your sister engaged?*

– *Yes, she will be married soon.*

– *Your cousin is chewing the cud.*

– *How is your cousin this morning?*

– *He is completely intoxicated.*

– *John is studying the psychology of the pimp.*

– *Was your sister sick last year?*

– *Yes, that was a case of food-poisoning. She had to be treated for constipation.*

– *Who is the big-shot in this city? Is it that ridiculous knight-errant?*

– *No. Nonetheless, he is the rubber-drive man.*

– *I would rather have a shorter life than be bald.*

Talking in Turkish

Anonymous (1990)

On holiday in Turkey a few years ago I found this little phrase book in a shop and seized on it with all the enthusiasm of a tourist and collector of mangled and misprinted English. It proved to be full of Turkish-English phrases endeavouring to cover every eventuality from making a journey by bus or train, to eating out in restaurants and even being able to cope with an unexpected visit to the dentist.

Here are just a few snippets...

– *You will find in it a choice of remarkable wonks.*

– *I have a request to do you.*

– *How much is it? I'll inke it.*

– *Do not talk on my back.*

– *I am very joyful to have been agreeable to you.*

– *Wait, it comes me an idea.*

– *Whose daughter is orying?*

– *Do you feel any drought?*

– *My nose is nearly frozen.*

– *You have become all pale, I have the quals.*

– *Excuse me, you ave wrong.*

– *What would you do if you were in my place?*

– *I would do so if I was in your plate.*

Lexicon Recentis Latinitatis

The Vatican (2003)

This huge Latin tome is probably the largest phrase book ever published. It consists of 23,000 terms spread over 728 tightly packed pages and makes fascinating reading for trivia searchers. Among the more bizarre entries must surely be *sideralis navis* for spaceship, *praecipua scaenica actrix* for a female television presenter, *capsellarum magnetoscopicarum* for a 'video rental shop' and the classic *pastillum botello fartum* to describe the humble 'hot dog'.

Over the years I have collected a number of other curious Latin translations from various books and they will, I think, provide quite enough 'wrotten English' for the time being!

Animus imbecillus – An idiotic animal.
Ave, domine – O Lord, I am a bird.
Aves alta petunt – The birds are getting high.
Caesar misit rotundas hominess – Caesar sent round men.
Corvi ovantes gutture – Crows laying eggs in the gutter.
Dulce satis humor – Enough of this sweet humour.
Felices ambo – We all love cats.
In hemicyclio sedentem, ut solebat – Ride a bicycle in order to get warm.
Nulli secundus – Next to nothing.
Pascebatque suas quisque senator oves – Every senator lived on his own eggs.
Plebs venit ac virides passim disjecta per herbas potat – The crowd lounged everywhere drinking through green straws.
Receptui cecinit – To sing at a reception.
Sardi venales – Sardines for sale.
Splendide mendax – A first-class liar.
Testudine acta – The tortoise is playing up.
Turpis sine frondibus arbor – A tree is disgraceful without leaves.
Vernit servus tristi vultu – The slave came with a sorrowful vulture.
Vinum amno – I love Venus.
Vomeere findis humum – You are flattening the ground with your stomach.

TEN

THE TOWER OF DRIVEL

A Blacklist of Critics' Clangers

Buried in a cemetery at Selborne in Hampshire are the last remains of a critic named Earp whose thoughtless – or perhaps just careless – parents gave him the initials TW. Although there is little evidence to suppose that he was anything other than a quietly spoken, self-effacing man dedicated to his work, his name became the inspiration for the term 'Twerp', meaning a foolish person. Earp was a friend of JRR Tolkien and at the university was known as a charming and witty man who belonged to all the art and literary societies. According to one account of his life by Romilly John, he 'took his lack of ambition to the extreme of becoming a critic'. Unlike all of those whose names and words appear in this chapter, however, the unfortunately named TW Earp never delivered a harsh or unkind criticism in his life.

It was the English journalist and wit Sir Sydney Smith who wrote, 'I never read a book before reviewing it; it prejudices a man so.' Benjamin Disraeli, the British Prime Minister and author of several truly awful novels, was just as set in his opinion, famously declaring, 'When I want to read a good book, I write one.'

There are very few things that people have been wrong about as often as they have been wrong about books. In this respect I am reminded of one of the highest awards for authors, the Nobel Prize for Literature, which has time and again overlooked great writers. Even when it was first launched in 1901 with such famous men as Henrik Ibsen, Émile Zola, Henry James and Joseph Conrad in their prime, the committee awarded the prize to René Sully-Prudhomme. René Sully-Prudhomme? Things got no better in the next few years with the award going to Theodor Mommsen, Bjonstjerne Bjornson and Frédéric Mistral, a French poet who wrote only in the Provençal dialect. It was not until

1907 that one of the truly great authors was awarded a Nobel Prize – Rudyard Kipling.

In the pages that follow are a selection of critics' clangers and unconstructive advice: voices raised in print against works the writers have adjudged worthless – often very amusingly so – but which time has proved the opposite. Those who were slated have, of course, all had the last laugh...

Nothing odd will do long.

Samuel Johnson on *Tristram Shandy*
by Laurence Sterne

———

So outrageously offensive to reason and common sense that one is naturally led to wonder how it can have been tolerated by a people amongst who astronomy, navigation and chemistry are understood.

William Cobbett on *Paradise Lost* by John Milton

———

His principles are ludicrously wicked and his poetry a melange of nonsense, cockneyism, poverty and pedantry.

Charles Lamb on *Prometheus Unbound* by
Percy Shelley

Tearing down all shreds of modesty, past all sense of
manliness and shame; filthy in word, filthy in
thought, furious, raging, obscene.

William M Thackeray on *Gulliver's Travels* by
Jonathan Swift

—•—

It might have been written by a seamstress who had
eaten something too rich for supper and slept upon
her back.

Jane Carlyle on *Isabella* by John Keats

—•—

I wish her characters would talk a little less like the
heroes and heroines of police reports.

George Eliot on *Jane Eyre* by Charlotte Brontë

—•—

All the faults of *Jane Eyre* are magnified a thousand-
fold and the only consolation which we have in
reflecting upon it is that it will never be
generally read.

James Lorimer on *Wuthering Heights* by
Emily Brontë

Another damned thick, square book! Always
scribble, scribble, scribble!

William Henry on *Decline and Fall of the
Roman Empire* by Edward Gibbon

I found out in the first two pages that it was a
woman's writing – she supposed
that in making a door, you last of all put
in the panels!

Thomas Carlyle on *Adam Bede* by George Eliot

One must have a heart of stone to read the death of
Little Nell without laughing.

Oscar Wilde on *The Old Curiosity Shop* by
Charles Dickens

If the author cannot think of something better to tell
our pure-minded lads and lasses, he had better stop
writing for them.

Louisa May Alcott on *Huckleberry Finn* by
Mark Twain

—•—

His work is evil and he is one of those unhappy beings of whom one can say that it would be better had he never been born.

Anatole France on *La Terre* by Émile Zola

—•—

In a hundred years the histories of French literature will only mention it as a curio.

Émile Zola on *Les Fleurs du Mal* by
Charles Baudelaire

—•—

It is not good enough to spend time and ink in describing the penultimate sensations and physical movements of people getting into a state of rut, we all know them too well.

John Galsworthy on *Sons and Lovers* by
D H Lawrence

—•—

We fancy any real child might be more puzzled than enchanted by this stiff, overwrought story.

James Lister on *Alice in Wonderland* by
Lewis Carroll

In Ireland they try to make a cat clean by rubbing its nose in its own filth. Mr Joyce has tried the same treatment on the human subject. I hope it may prove successful.

George Bernard Shaw on *Ulysses* by James Joyce

Juvenile trash.

Edmund Wilson on *The Lord of the Rings* by
J R R Tolkien

No, no, this kind of thing won't do. The good folks below (I mean posterity) will have none of it.

James Lowell on *Leaves of Grass* by Walt Whitman

This work is so helpless, so crude, so bad, so clumsily feeble and vulgar.

Henry James on *An Ideal Husband* by Oscar Wilde

———

It seemed to me that the man who wrote it had a mind like a sewer. There were few people in this fictional place whose thoughts did not dwell most of the time on booze or lechery or both.

George Murray on *Under Milk Wood* by Dylan Thomas

———

A grunt would serve equally well.

J C Squire on *The Waste Land* by T S Eliot

———

A huge dose of hyperbolic slang, maudlin sentimentalism and tragic-comic bubble-and-squeak.

William H Ainsworth on *Moby Dick* by Herman Melville

———

It is that word 'hummy', my darlings, that marks the first place at which Tonstant Weader Fwowed up.

Dorothy Parker on *The House at Pooh Corner* by
A A Milne

It would be useless to pretend that it would be very widely read.

Ford Madox Ford on *Heart of Darkness* by
Joseph Conrad

The final blow-up of what was once a remarkable, if minor, talent.

Clifton Fadiman on *Absalom, Absalom* by
William Faulkner

The physical details, both in lascivious description and implication are disgusting. As to its literary value, I can see none.

Vita Sackville-West on *Lolita* by Vladimir Nabokov

The petty, cowardly, mean and philistine character of the doctor is as alien to the Soviet people as is the malignant literary snob who wrote this book.

V Semichastny on *Doctor Zhivago* by Boris Pasternak

From the moment I picked up your book until I laid it down I was convulsed with laughter. Someday I intend to read it.

Groucho Marx on *Dawn Ginsbergh's Revenge* by S J Perelman

It is a failure.

Laurence Brander on *Nineteen Eighty-Four* by George Orwell

I would rather put a phial of prussic acid into the hands of a healthy boy or girl than the book in question.

James Douglas on *The Well of Loneliness* by Radclyffe Hall

The book turned out to be a work both disgraceful and scandalous. It abounds in coarse and sometimes disgusting passages and its climax is disgusting. We refuse to print its title or to mention its publishers.

Ernest Oldmeadown on *Black Mischief* by Evelyn Waugh

Readers less easily thrown off their trolley will still prefer Hans Andersen.

R W Lewis on *Of Mice and Men* by John Steinbeck

This rather nasty, rather pompous novel gives us, in all, a precocious small boy's view of life, the boy having been spoiled somehow and allowed to indulge in sulks and tantrums and abundant self-pity.

Walter Inskip on *The Ginger Man* by J P Donleavy

It is only fair to the author to remark on the utter
lack of decorum of any kind in this dreadful little
volume. The title is meant to be a noun, but I can't
help taking it as an imperative.

John Hollander on *Howl* by Allen Ginsberg

Not only is there no word or suggestion of the
romantic, sentimental, poetic or spiritual aspects of
the sex relation, but it is not even bawdy sex, or
comic sex, or sex described with good humour. No
glory, no beauty, no stars – just mud.

Thomas Desmond on *Tropic of Cancer* by
Henry Miller

The merest trash, not worth a look.

Arthur Forsythe on *Naked Lunch* by
William Burroughs

It's a fake – a clever, talented, admirably
executed fake.

Gore Vidal on *The Naked and the Dead* by
Norman Mailer

The author wallows in his own laughter and finally drowns in it. What remains is a debris of sour jokes, stage anger, dirty words, synthetic looniness and the sort of antic behaviour the children fall into when they know they are losing our attention.

Whitney Balliett on *Catch-22* by Joseph Heller

Certainly America has something better to offer the world, along with its arms and its armies, than such a confession of spiritual vacuum as this.

Ambrose Elliott on *From Here to Eternity* by James Jones

If I were asked to point to a passage which combined all that prose fiction should not be – lurid sentimentality, preposterous morals, turgid and sticky style – I do not think I could point to anything worse than the closing chapters of this book.

Edmund Gosse on *Howards End* by E M Forster

From time to time it's nice to have a book you can hate – it clears the pipes – and I hate this book.

Peter Prescott on *Breakfast of Champions* by Kurt Vonnegut

A farce that is continually over-reaching itself. Or, as the Cheyenne might put it, Little Big Man Little Overblown.

Gerald Walker on *Little Big Man* by Thomas Berger

The story is too improbable to arouse interest, nor do I like the underlying atmosphere of violence, luxury and lust. I regard it as an obscene book 'liable to corrupt'.

Harold Nicolson on *Goldfinger* by Ian Fleming

One can say of this book – with sufficient truth to make it worth saying: 'This isn't writing. It's research.'

Stanley Kauffman on *In Cold Blood* by Truman Capote

This book was apparently completed in Cuba in 1960
and, for all the good it is likely to do the author's
reputation, it could well have stayed
there – permanently.

Geoffrey Wagner on *A Moveable Feast* by
Ernest Hemingway

I believe that on the evidence of this book there is
little to say except that a good wage, accessible sex
and a telly aren't everything. Any Sunday-school
teacher could have made the point in fewer words.

Fred Majdalany on *Saturday Night and Sunday
Morning* by Alan Sillitoe

The book itself is inaccurate in detail and fraudulent
in method to the point of being very bad. The reason
these things were not detected by the reviewers is
that it said what they wanted to hear.

Martin Green on *The Outsider* by Colin Wilson

For the reader who has put away comic books, but isn't ready for the editorial in the *Daily News*.

Gloria Steinem on *Valley of the Dolls* by
Jacqueline Susann

He is a good writer, but I wouldn't want to shake hands with him.

Jacqueline Susann on *Portnoy's Complaint* by
Philip Roth

That this wretched, drivelling affair, its impressions fuzzy with jet lag and neutral-flavoured as an airline meal, should have been made into a bestseller, with all the attendant flimflam of the hired train and 8.2 autographed copies per minute, is a signpost towards the gap between those who buy books and those who read them.

Jonathan Keats on *Travels* by Edward Heath

ELEVEN

Dying is the Last Thing
I Want to Do

A Literary Graveyard of Final Words

Writers have evidently been as keen as anyone among the great and the good to leave a final admonition for posterity. Whether these last words have been especially written to be read after death, committed to a letter or diary, or just imparted on their deathbeds, many have proved revealing and not a few rather amusing. Of course, some authors said nothing, while others of whom greater things might be expected failed to rise to the occasion.

Thomas Gray, of *Elegy in a Country Churchyard* fame, breathed his last in 1771 with, 'Molly, I shall die,' while the great Samuel Johnson similarly addressed a relative – in his case, his step-daughter – some twelve years later with, 'God Bless you, my dear.' A century on, the French writer George Sand (Amandine Dupon) was a little more fulsome to her family: 'Farewell, I am going to die. Goodbye Lina, goodbye Maurice, goodbye Lolo, good . . .' Then, sadly, she ran out of breath, literally. Another Frenchman, the grammarian Dominique Bouhours, remained true to his profession right to the very end, declaring on his deathbed in 1702: 'I am about to, or, I am going to, die. Either expression is used.' Best of all, though, I like the story the writer John Mortimer used to tell of his father, Clifford. The old man's last words were, 'I'm always angry when I'm dying.'

The writers' words quoted in this chapter are taken from a variety of sources from the written to the oral and in many instances are as amusing, satirical and interesting as the people themselves had been in life. The expression which so ideally heads this chapter is attributed to the great American actor, John Barrymore, who died in 1942.

Epicurus (c. 540–450 BC)

Greek teacher and philosopher who is said to have written over 300 volumes expounding his belief that pleasure was the chief good, of which only one, *Volumina Herculanensia*, has survived.

'Now, farewell, and remember all my words!'

Chrysippus (c. 280–207 BC)

Greek philosopher who lived and worked in Athens and is also believed to have been a prolific writer, of which just a few humorous fragments remain.

'Go and give the ass a drink of wine to wash down the figs.'

Niccolò Machiavelli (1469–1527)

Italian author who wrote a number of historical studies, as well as the controversial *The Prince* (published after his death, in 1532) which advocated treachery as a means of successful government and was banned by Pope Clement VIII.

'I desire to go to hell and not to heaven. In the former place I shall enjoy the company of Popes, Kings and Princes, while in the latter are only beggars, monks and apostles.'

Pietro Aretino (1492–1557)

Italian poet and adventurer whose controversial verses, the *Sonetti Lussuriosi* (c. 1524), earned him a reputation for impudent wit and the epithet 'the scourge of princes'.

'Keep the rats away now that I'm all greased up.'

François Rabelais (1494–1553)

French satirist who briefly followed careers in the church and medicine before writing a series of riotous, comic masterpieces including *Gargantua* (1532) and *Pantagruel* (1533).

'*Ring down the curtain, the farce is over.*'

George Buchanan (1506–82)

Scottish reformer and writer who was imprisoned for his satirical poem, 'Franciscanus' (1539), directed against the church, and renowned for his outspoken history of insurgency among the Scots lords, *Detectio Mariae Reginae* (1562).

'*They may leave my corpse to rot where I die if they wish!*'

Miguel de Cervantes (1547–1616)

Spanish author, soldier and prisoner of war who was ransomed by monks and went on to create one of the great masterpieces of literature, *Don Quixote* (1605).

'*Already my foot is in the stirrup.*'

Nicolas Boileau (1636–1711)

French critic whose early satires brought him into trouble with the establishment, but who was ultimately acclaimed for his study, *L'Art Poétique* (1674).

'*It is a great consolation to a dying poet to have never written anything against morality.*'

William Wycherley (1640–1716)

English dramatist and man about town who became famous for *Love In A Wood* (1671) and *The Country Wife* (1675) and notorious when he took a young wife at the age of 65.

'My dear, you will never marry an old man again!'

Daniel Defoe (1660–1731)

English author whose extraordinary life as a traveller, rebel and government spy inspired his later writings, including the immortal *Robinson Crusoe* (1720) and his roistering tale of low life, *Moll Flanders* (1722).

'I do not know which is more difficult in a Christian life – to live well or to die well!'

Jonathan Swift (1667–1745)

Dublin-born satirist who came to public notice with *Battle of the Books* (1704), but achieved immortality with *Gulliver's Travels* in 1726 – complete with its disguised attack on political parties and religious dissension.

'I am dying like a poisoned rat in a hole – I am what I am!'

Andrew Bradford (1686–1742)

American writer and in 1719 founder of one of the first magazines in the new colony, the *American Weekly Mercury*, he was later imprisoned for defending the freedom of the press.

'Oh, Lord, forgive the errata!'

Alexander Pope (1688–1744)

English satirist, poet and precocious critic of contemporary literature, who found fame in 1712 with *The Rape of the Lock*.

'I am dying, sir, of one hundred good symptoms.'

Richard Brinsley Sheridan (1751–1816)

Irish-born dramatist and parliamentarian whose hugely popular plays *The Rivals (*1775) and *School for Scandal* (1777) were not sufficient to prevent him from dying in great poverty.

'I am absolutely undone.'

Robert Burns (1759–96)

Scottish poet who contributed some of the most beautiful, passionate and tender verses in any language including 'Tam o' Shanter' and 'Holy Willie's Prayer'.

'Don't let the awkward squad fire over me.'

William Wordsworth (1770–1850)

English poet whose lifelong love of nature was exemplified in his collections of verse and offset his troubled life and the mental breakdown of his wife, Dorothy.

'Is that you, Dora?'

Sir Walter Scott (1771–1832)

Scottish law clerk who became one of his nation's most famous writers
as a result of his series of Waverley novels that mixed country life with
high adventure and ranged from *A Legend of Montrose* (1819) to *The
Talisman* (1825).

'I have written nothing which on my deathbed I should wish blotted.'

Samuel Taylor Coleridge (1772–1834)

English essayist, critic and poet famous for his verses, notably 'The
Rime of the Ancient Mariner' (1798) and 'Kubla Khan' (1816).

*'A handsome legacy for that most faithful, affectionate and
disinterested servant Harriet Macklin.'*

Charles Lamb (1775–1834)

English essayist noted for his reckless humour and wild fun that
alternated between tenderness and profound philosophy, as
demonstrated in collections like *The Last Essays of Elia* (1833).

'My bedfellows are cramp and cough – we three all in one bed!'

Washington Irving (1783–1859)

American novelist whose early work burlesqued the old Dutch settlers
in New York, but who achieved lasting fame with *The Sketch Book*
(1819–20), which contained the immortal stories of 'The Legend of
Sleepy Hollow' and 'Rip Van Winkle'.

'Well, I must arrange my pillows for another night – when will this end!'

Mary Russell Mitford (1787–1855)

English daughter of a spendthrift physician who turned to writing to support her family and won acclaim for her stories of country life collected as *Our Village* (1832).

'If you wish for another cheerful evening with your old friend, there is no time to be lost.'

Lord George Byron (1788–1824)

Dissipated English poet and 'man of mystery' whose grand tour of Spain, Albania, Greece and the Aegean produced his classic work, *Childe Harold's Pilgrimage* (1812).

'The damned doctors have drenched me so that I can scarcely stand.'

Heinrich Heine (1797–1856)

German author and poet who failed as a banker and doctor before achieving fame as a lyrical and polemical writer with *Das Buch der Lieder [Book of Songs]* (1827).

'God will pardon me – it's His profession.'

Jules Michelet (1798–1874)

French historian who worked in the Paris Records Office before publishing his monumental 24-volume, *Histoire de France* (1833–67) which he then followed with seven volumes on the French Revolution.

'Do you know what linen is? Linen is a great thing – I want to make a book of it!'

Thomas Hood (1799–1845)

English humorist whose popular series of *Whims and Oddities* (1826) led to his editorship of *Hood's Monthly Magazine*. He died curiously, while a mustard plaster was being applied to one of his feet.

'There's very little meat for the mustard.'

Thomas Lovell Beddoes (1803–49)

English poet and physiologist who led a strange peripatetic life as a doctor in Europe until his work *The Bride's Tragedy* (1822) was followed by the even greater success of *Death's Jest Book* in 1849.

'I am food for what I am good for – worms.'

Elizabeth Barrett Browning (1806–61)

English poet who wrote a moving epic, *The Battle of Marathon*, while she was only fourteen and later became famous for the heartfelt story of *Aurora Leigh* (1856).

'Beautiful!'

Charles Dickens (1812–70)

English journalist, magazine editor and novelist of innumerable classics including *Martin Chuzzlewit* (1843*), David Copperfield* (1850) *and Little Dorrit* (1857).

'Be natural – for the writer that is natural has fulfilled all the rules of the art.'

Edward Lear (1812–88)

English artist and author whose enduring fame was assured by his illustrated collection of comic verse, *Book of Nonsense* (1846), and its three sequels.

'I did not answer the letters of my friends because I could not write, as no sooner did I take a pen in my hand than I felt as if I was dying.'

Walt Whitman (1819–92)

American poet whose controversial work *Leaves of Grass* (1855) was labelled 'an indecent book' because of its focus on male love, a taboo subject at the time.

'Oh, dear, he's a good fellow.'

Anne Brontë (1820–49)

English governess and member of the famous family of writers, who under her pseudonym, Acton Bell, wrote *The Tenant of Wildfell Hall* (1848).

'Take courage! Take courage!'

Alice Cary (1820–71)

American poet and storyteller who spent much of her life travelling across America and writing about her experiences and wrote the famous hymn, 'One Sweetly Solemn Thought' with her younger sister, Phoebe.

'I want to go away.'

Alfred Williams (1828–1905)

English poet and translator of the ancient manuscript, *The Panchatantra* (c. 200 BC), which included the subsequently much-anthologised stories, 'Leap and Creep' and 'The Three-Breasted Princess'.

'My dear, this is going to be a tragedy for us both.'

Jules Verne (1828–88)

French 'Father of Science Fiction' whose prophetic novels *Voyage to the Centre of the Earth* (1864), *From the Earth to the Moon* (1869) and *Twenty Thousand Leagues Under the Sea* (1870) inspired a genre and generations of later writers.

'Are you there?'

Louisa May Alcott (1832–88)

American writer of children's stories that began with *Little Women* in 1868 and was followed by several sequels, which have delighted countless young readers ever since.

'Is this not meningitis?'

Mark Twain (1835–1910)

American writer and humorist, born Samuel Langhorne Clemens, who was a printer, riverboat pilot and gold miner before achieving fame with the stories of Huckleberry Finn.

'I came in with Halley's comet and I will go out with it.'

Thomas Bailey Aldrich (1836–1907)

American poet, novelist, editor of the *Atlantic Monthly* and author of a bestseller, *The Story of a Bad Boy* (1870), based on his childhood in New Hampshire.

'In spite of it all, I'm going to sleep.'

Émile Zola (1840–1902)

French novelist of the *document humain* that focused on the underbelly of French life in novels such as *Nana* (1880) and *Germinal* (1885). Tragically, he was suffocated by charcoal fumes.

'I feel sick. The dog is sick, too. We are both ill. It must be something we have eaten.'

Ambrose Bierce (1842–1914?)

American writer of sardonic fiction including *In the Midst of Life* (1892) and *Can Such Things Be?* (1893) who disappeared while travelling in Mexico after writing these words.

'To be a gringo in Mexico – ah, that is euthanasia!'

Anatole France (1844–1924)

French writer who began his literary career writing publishers' blurbs and rose to fame with satirical novels such as *Les Opinions de Jerome Coignard* (1893).

'So this is what it is like to die – it takes a long time!'

Paul Verlaine (1844–96)

French poet and short-story writer whose life of penury and imprisonment was reflected in volumes such as *Poèmes Saturniens* (1867) *and Élégies* (1893).

'Don't sole the dead man's shoes yet!'

Joel Chandler Harris (1848–1908)

American author who worked as a lawyer and journalist until his comic masterpiece, *Uncle Remus* (1880), made him and his character, Brer Rabbit, world famous.

'I am about the extent of a tenth of a gnat's eyebrow better.'

Sir William Nicoll (1851–1923)

Scottish writer who gave up being a church minister in Kelso to settle in London as an editor and writer on theology and literature for the *Expositor*.

'I believe everything I have written about immortality.'

Oscar Wilde (1854–1900)

Irish wit, poet and dramatist whose notorious life and mastery of the epigram almost overshadow his great works including *A Woman of No Importance* (1894) and *The Importance of Being Earnest* (1899).

'I am dying as I have lived – beyond my means.'

Frank Harris (1856–1931)

Irish-born journalist, incorrigible liar, vociferous boaster and philanderer whose autobiography, *My Life and Loves* (1923–7) was banned for indecency.

   'Nellie, my Nellie, I'm going!'

George Bernard Shaw (1856–1950)

Irish novelist, dramatist and critic who worked for a firm of land agents before devoting himself to literature and was propelled to fame by his great philosophical comedy, *Man and Superman* (1902).

   'Sister, you are trying to keep me alive as an old curiosity.'

Joseph Conrad (1857–1924)

Polish-born son of a revolutionary who was a merchant seaman for ten years before becoming a famous writer with his novels *Lord Jim* (1900), *Nostromo* (1904) and *Chance* (1914).

   'I am better this morning. I can always get a rise out of you, Jess...'

Sir Arthur Conan Doyle (1859–1930)

Scottish novelist who suffered poverty as a young doctor until his creation of the immortal detective Sherlock Holmes in 1887 in *A Study in Scarlet* made him wealthy and enduringly famous.

   'You are wonderful.'

Anton Chekhov (1860–1904)

Russian author who began writing comic essays as a student – later published as *Motley Stories* (1886) – but achieved fame as a playwright with several timeless classics including *Uncle Vanya* (1900) and *The Cherry Orchard* (1904).

'I haven't drunk champagne for a long time.'

J M Barrie (1860–1937)

Scottish novelist and dramatist who wrote stories of rural life until the extraordinary success of his social satire, *The Admiral Crichton* (1902), followed by the immortal *Peter Pan* in 1904.

'I can't sleep.'

O Henry (1862–1910)

American short-story writer who was charged with fraud and fled to Central America, but returned to become a writer in New York, where his tales with an unexpected twist – such as *The Four Million* (1906) – made him famous.

'Turn up the lights – I don't want to go home in the dark.'

William Butler Yeats (1865–1939)

Irish writer and poet whose book *The Celtic Twilight* (1893) launched a renaissance of ancient Irish culture and inspired a whole new school of playwrights and poets.

'You can refute Hegel, but not the Saint or the Song of Sixpence.'

H G Wells (1866–1946)

English writer, journalist and prophet whose novels, including *The Time Machine* (1895), *War of the Worlds* (1898) and *The Shape of Things to Come* (1933), have proved hugely influential on the science fiction genre.

'Go away – I'm all right!'

Luigi Pirandello (1867–1936)

Italian novelist and short-story writer who became famous for his 'grotesque' dramas, including *Six Characters in Search of an Author* (1920), and who won the Nobel Prize for Literature.

'The hearse, the horse, the driver and – enough!'

Arnold Bennett (1867–1931)

English novelist who began his working life in a solicitor's office but later wrote a series of novels about the 'Five Towns' (the Potteries area around Stoke-on-Trent) as well as a number of humorous stories including *The Grand Babylon Hotel* (1902) and *The Card* (1911).

'Everything has gone wrong, my girl!'

Edwin Arlington Robinson (1869–1935)

American poet who won the Pulitzer Prize three times and was widely admired for his novels, notably *The Man Who Died Twice* (1925).

'We'll have our cigarettes together.'

André Gide (1869–1951)

French writer and Nobel prize-winner for his fiction, poetry and plays including the influential *L'Immoraliste* (1902), and his autobiography, *Si le Grain ne Meurt* (1920).

'*C'est bien.*'

Hector Munro ('Saki') (1870–1916)

British novelist who became famous as a satirist of the upper-class Edwardian world of England with *The Unbearable Bassington* (1912) and *Beasts and Superbeasts* (1914) but died tragically by a sniper's bullet while serving in the First World War.

'*Put that bloody cigarette out!*'

Robert Hugh Benson (1871–1914)

English preacher and novelist, author of *Come Rack! Come Rope!* (1921) and the famous ghost story 'The Watcher' (1903).

'*Arthur! Don't look at me. Nurse! Stand between my brother and I!*'

Marcel Proust (1871–1922)

French novelist whose semi-invalid life and passion for introspection produced his seemingly endless work, *A la Recherche du Temps Perdu* (Remembrance of Times Past, 1913–22).

'*I shall stop now. I can't go on.*'

W Somerset Maugham (1874–1965)

English novelist who qualified as a surgeon and used his experiences in the two world wars to produce a series of classic novels including *Of Human Bondage* (1915), *Of Cakes and Ale* (1930) and *The Razor's Edge* (1945).

'Dying is a very dull, dreary affair and my advice to you is to have nothing whatever to do with it.'

James Joyce (1882–1941)

Irish writer who left Ireland when young but used his native city as the inspiration for a collection of short stories, *Dubliners* (1914), and for his most complex and controversial novel, *Ulysses*, first published in Paris in 1922.

'Does nobody understand?'

Ben Travers (1886–1980)

English novelist and playwright who was a master of the light farce and delighted generations of playgoers with productions such as *A Cuckoo in the Nest* (1925).

'This is where the real fun starts.'

Marguerite Radclyffe Hall (1880–1943)

English novelist whose *Adam's Breed* (1926) won the *Femina Vie Heureuse* and was followed by her sympathetic study of lesbianism, *The Well of Loneliness* (1928), which was banned for years in Britain.

'What a life!'

Alexander Woollcott (1887–1943)

American journalist, broadcaster and short-story writer who is remembered for his larger than life personality and influence on popular tastes.

'I have no need of your Goddamned sympathy – I want to be entertained by some of your grosser reminiscences.'

Donn Byrne (1889–1928)

Irish-American novelist who worked as a cowpuncher in South America, as a garage mechanic in New York and wrote several bestsellers including *Hangman's House* (1926) before dying in a motoring accident.

'I think I'll go for a drive before dinner – anyone coming?'

George S Kaufman (1889–1961)

American humorist and playwright famous for his wit in *The Butter and Egg Man* (1925) and his collaboration with Moss Hart, *You Can't Take It With You* (1936).

'I'm not afraid any more.'

Robert Benchley (1889–1945)

American humorist whose gently sardonic writings were collected in volumes such as *My Ten Years in a Quandary* (1936). He died reading a book called *Am I Thinking?* after writing on the title page:

'No. And supposing you were?'

Dorothy Parker (1893–1967)

American writer famous for her biting wit and satiric humour as exemplified in her collections of verse such as *Enough Rope* (1927) and short stories, *Laments for the Living* (1930) and *Here Lies* (1939).

'Excuse my dust.'

e e cummings (1894–1962)

American writer of essays and poems whose rhythm and style, often omitting capital letters, were seen to great effect in collections such as *The Enormous Room* (1922) and *Eimi* (1933).

'I'm going to stop now – but I'm going to sharpen the axe before I put it up.'

James Thurber (1894–1964)

American journalist and author whose hugely popular comic and satirical books, illustrated by himself, included *Is Sex Necessary?* (1929) and *The Thurber Album* (1952).

'God Bless...Goddamn!'

F Scott Fitzgerald (1896–1940)

American novelist who lived through the rampant hedonism of the 'Jazz Age' and captured its spirit in *The Beautiful and the Damned* (1922), *The Great Gatsby* (1925) and *The Last Tycoon* (1941).

'Hershey bars will be good enough – they'll be fine.'

Bertolt Brecht (1898–1956)

German dramatist who captured the bawdy and the sublime on paper
to make his reputation with *Dreigroschenoper* [The Threepenny Opera]
(1928), an adaptation of the *Beggar's Opera*.

*'At least one knows that death will be easy – a slight knock at the
windowpane, then...'*

Thomas Wolfe (1900–1938)

American novelist whose ambitious project for a series of six related
novels was cut short by pneumonia, although his reputation was
assured by the first book, *Look Homeward, Angel* (1929).

'All right, Mabel, I am coming.'

George Orwell (1903–50)

English novelist who fought in the Spanish Civil War and became a
fiery socialist as well as a satirist and made his name with the brilliant
Animal Farm (1945) and prophetic *Nineteen Eighty-Four* (1949).

'At fifty, everyone has the face that he deserves.'

Dylan Thomas (1914–53)

Welsh poet and writer whose talent was revealed in *Portrait of the
Artist as a Young Dog* (1940) and *Under Milk Wood* (1954), but whose
reputation was ensured by his riotous, drunken lifestyle.

*'I've had eighteen straight whiskies. I think that's the record. After 39
years, this is all I've done.'*

Allen Ginsberg (1926–97)

American poet and angry radical who was one of the leading lights of the 'Beat Generation' and wrote one of its most famous poems, 'Howl', in 1956.

'I am quite happy – unaccountably happy!'

Spike Milligan (1918–2003)

Irish author and scriptwriter who co-wrote and performed in *The Goon Show* in 1951, and wrote a number of bestselling books, including a comic gem, *Puckoon* (1963) and a series of 'autobiographies' about his military service, which began with *Adolf Hitler: My Part in His Downfall* (1971). This is his epitaph:

'I told you I was ill.'

Finally, I must just make room for a remark by the great American comedian, scriptwriter and novelist, Woody Allen. Although still very much with us, Woody has already prepared his epitaph:

'It's not that I'm afraid to die. I just don't want to be there when it happens.'

ERRATA

Publishers' Boobs and Apologies

A Gallimaufry of Book Trade Errors

The unprecedented success of *Eats, Shoots and Leaves*, Lynn Truss's book about the vagaries and abuses of the English language, has brought into focus the errors to which writers and publishers are prone. When her little volume began scaling the bestseller lists in 2003, I was reminded of a publisher's advertisement that appeared in an American newspaper in Indiana in the 1960s announcing the publication of a book on punctuation. The ad read: 'Revised and enlarged Rules of Punction, a valuable, easy-to-understand text for writers, secretaries and students. For a copy send a stamped, self-addressed envelope marked punciation booklet.' Two errors for the price of one!

This final chapter is devoted to a pot-pourri of mistakes featuring writers and publishers, along with some of the errors that have bedevilled reviewers of books, and where better to begin an assortment of errors and misprints than with a letter to *The Times* written in 1965 by C R Edgeley, the manager of The Times Book Company Ltd:

'Sir, How carefully do people read? The question arises out of a recent experience here. Not until a copy of a novel of high literary merit had reached its thirteenth reader was it noticed that a whole section of the book had been erroneously inserted and was, indeed, part of an entirely different book. It is all the more surprising in that, at the point where the wrong insertion is made, the last page of the correct book ended halfway through a sentence, and the first page of the wrong book began a new chapter. The characters and setting were also entirely different.'

Easy to Learn Chess published by Max Parrish in 1965 may not have proved quite so easy to readers who were baffled by this explanation at the start of the book:

Chess is a game of skill, played by two four smaller squares of equal size, coloured persons on a square board divided into sixty – alternately light and dark.

—•—

Two years later, another London publisher, Macdonald & Co., found themselves in a similarly embarrassing situation when they issued *A Textbook on Climbing*:

In climbing, the principal cause of fatigue of the arms is the lack of circulation due to their being held above the head continuously. The feet seldom suffer in this way.

—•—

Following the publication in 1977 of the *Easy Sky Diving Book*, the publishers Warrenton Fauquier of Virginia issued a rather alarming press statement and an insert for every copy of the book. It read:

On page eight, line seven, the words 'state zip code' should read – 'pull rip cord'.

—•—

The publishers of the 1978 edition of *Dod's Parliamentary Companion* were also forced to print the following Correction with all copies:

Reference to Lord Gibson's biography on page 122: for 'National Front' read NATIONAL TRUST.

—•—

In 1991, the *Reader's Digest* told the extraordinary story of a glossy American cookbook which contained a recipe for Silky Caramel Slice. The instructions stated, 'Put an unopened can of condensed milk in a pot and leave on the stove for four hours.' The *Digest* report continued:

The publishers later recalled all the books at vast expense when they realised they had just invented the first exploding pudding. They had forgotten to mention that the pot should first be filled with water.

A rather unusual situation faced the *Business Times of Singapore* when one of their titles in a series of self-help books, *Business and the Arts,* was issued in 1989:

Some readers who called up about the blank space that appeared in one of our books published last week were inadvertently told to iron the spot and an etching of Ezra Pound would appear. The person who gave that instruction has since been chastised. It was actually a production slip-up. As such, claims for burnt pages and damaged irons will not be entertained.

According to a diary report in the *London Evening News* in 1967 concerning a number of errors found in a recently published book from a leading publishing company:

The publishers have promised to insert a slip in future editions acknowledging the sauce of passages quoted.

The Red Cross Society also had to apologise for a case of the obvious that slipped through in one of their first-aid manuals in 1968:

If the patient faints when standing up he collapses on to the ground.

An even more comic example of the same was reported in 1993 from a handbook issued by the European Parliament in Brussels:

There is a fundamental difference between male and female homosexuality, which is that the former concerns men and the second women.

A corrigendum slip appeared with the copies of the *Australian Dictionary of National Biography* in 2001 referring to page 168:

For 'died in infancy' read 'lived to a ripe old age at Orange'.

Hansard, which records the daily debates in the Houses of Parliament, noted in a totally straight-faced way in May 2003 what was surely the raciest House of Lords Amendment, under the heading 'Baroness Noakes and Lord Astor on the Sexual Offences Bill':

Page 32, line 1, leave out 'genitals', insert 'penis'.

The same august publication was also responsible for another no doubt similarly inadvertent bit of humour in its Index to the 1965 edition:

Seats – see under Members.

In 1931, the *Washington Post* reported the embarrassment of a local publisher who had issued a new title with the following lines underneath the author's photograph:

Words come easy to him – words that have a musical sway, words that come from an active mind, not marital words but those of peace.

A lively column known as 'Syndicalism' issued by the *American People's Book Series* picked up this comic extract in 1954:

Man now had his clothes stripped off, and was exposed, naked as when he was born, to the intrusive and penetrating gaze of his brother-man. He had to make new combinations.

In 1970, the editor of the trade magazine *World's Press News* launched a search to find the world's most prolific author. Under a headline, 'Challenge', he appealed:

We believe that Michael Hervey, author of 1,500 short stories, is the [most] prolific storywriter of all time. If any other writer, living or dead, has equalled this record we shall be pleased to hear from him.

The editor of the popular children's comic *Mickey Mouse Weekly* enthused to his young readers in 1959:

Who hasn't read Lewis Carroll's famous classic, and who doesn't love this fabulous fantasy? Everyone, I'm sure.

The Sunday Times committed an amusing misprint in its review for a book by Mary Constable in 1958:

She is a great believer in the importance of a child having real knowledge of the body instead of allowing it to be wrapped in mystery. She has accordingly included in the book an appendix giving clear details of its workings.

In 1969, the *London Evening Standard* contacted a number of celebrities to ask what books they were reading. Among these was the millionaire businessman, Charles Clore:

He has just finished Mario Puzo's novel, The Godfather, which discusses methods used by the Mafia. He was most interested.

Reviewing *The Bedside Guardian 21* in 1970, MP Reginald Maudling wrote:

I do not think that I am a very suitable person to review a bedside book, because my trouble has always been waking up rather than going to sleep.

Whether the publisher or author were more embarrassed over an entry in the Hutchinson & Co Catalogue in 1969 can only be imagined:

The book contains a portrait of the author and several other quaint illustrations.

Sidgwick & Jackson were also hit by a gremlin when publishing *The Professionals: Prostitutes and their Clients* by Iain Scarlet in 1971. Their catalogue stated:

The Professionals are Alice, Caroline, Jan, Danielle and Kathy: five women to whom prostitution is a business and a way of life. Simon and Joe are the cunters, the men for whom the girls exist.

In 1980, Duckworth provided a similarly unfortunate choice of words about one of their authors:

For more than fifteen years, Priscilla Elfrey has specialised in helping managers and executives perform more effectively on the job.

And just to prove that American publishers can make equally careless gaffes, the 1981 Houghton Mifflin Catalogue commented on one of its authors:

Lois Lowry is the author of three highly acclaimed children's books, A Summer To Die, which won the IRA Children's Book Award...